THE TRIAL OF
ABIGAIL
GOODMAN

Also by Howard Fast

THE TRIAL OF ABIGAIL GOODMAN

HOWARD FAST

CROWN PUBLISHERS, INC.
NEW YORK

Published by Crown Publishers, Inc., 201 East 50th Street,
New York, New York 10022. Member of the Crown Publishing Group.
Random House, Inc. New York, Toronto, London, Sydney, Auckland

CROWN is a trademark of Crown Publishers, Inc.

Manufactured in the United States of America

Library of Congress Cataloging-in-Publication Data

Fast, Howard
    The trial of Abigail Goodman : a novel / Howard Fast.—1st ed.
    1. Trials (Abortion)—Fiction.   I. Title.
    PS3511.A784T54   1993
    813'.52—dc20   93-18043
                                                          CIP

ISBN 0-517-59502-8

10 9 8 7 6 5 4 3 2 1

First Edition

Fic.

For Bette

My gratitude to

Barbara Grace Fast for her legal advice,
Dr. Norman Herzig for his medical assistance,
Sterling Lord for his patience and persistence.

THE TRIAL OF
ABIGAIL
GOODMAN

1

June 11. Julia Hyde, City Press Syndicate:

Today marks the first courtroom appearance of Professor Abigail
Goodman, accused of murder. The trial will take place here in
Clarkton, the county center, in the Clarkton Courthouse, which,
it should be noted, is one of the sixteen public buildings in the
state that have been singled out for preservation as landmark
structures.

The courthouse was designed by Addison Graves, the best-
known of the antebellum architects, in 1856. Its construction
was interrupted by the Civil War, but the plans were not dis-
carded, and it was completed in 1873. With its pillared front

and broad steps, it overwhelms the rest of the town. It stands at one side of the town square, facing a bandstand and a monument to the fallen Confederate soldiers. One enters up an approach of twenty stone steps.

On this morning, eight policemen are on duty in front of the courthouse, and a dozen more cover two demonstrations taking place in the park, one a demonstration in support of the accused, a crowd of about thirty people, mostly women, all of them hastily bussed in from out of town; the other demonstration consisting mostly of local people, men and women, waving strident signs that proclaim their position. Their position states very simply and directly that Abigail Goodman is guilty of murder, first the verdict, then the trial.

The media has taken over the steps to the courthouse. There are six television trucks, a whole battery of microphones and cameras lining the approach, male reporters, female reporters, a chorus of voices in southern English, middle Atlantic, French accents, German accents, British accents, a babble of voices to underline the fact that the whole world has discovered Clarkton and is ready to see and hear and comment on a very extraordinary trial.

The Clarkton County district attorney, who will prosecute the case against Abigail Goodman, makes no claim to impartiality. He ran on the Republican ticket and was elected with the strong support of the local Chamber of Commerce. His name is Charles Anderson. The case will be heard by Judge George Lee Benson, superior court judge for the district.

While Professor Goodman's husband, William, is an attorney, the Goodmans have hired the husband-and-wife team of Jack and Button Ridley for Professor Goodman's defense. Mr. Goodman will act as co-counsel.

According to Millicent Woolton, in charge of public relations for the Goodmans, the Goodmans have received numerous offers from distinguished out-of-state attorneys to take part in the case. They have not yet determined whether or not they will take advantage of any of the offers, although several of them are pro bono. The Ridleys have a reputation as civil rights lawyers.

Abigail Goodman's family, the Hendersons, have lived for generations in Clarkton. Her grandfather, Floyd Henderson, was a United States senator—a fact that seems to win Professor Goodman little sympathy from the local citizens, a resentment that stems in part from the fact that she had moved to the northern part of the state—where she is a tenured professor at the prestigious Hilden College—and had married a New York–born Jew.

The Goodmans were in Clarkton, taking care of the sale of her grandmother's house and the disposition of the Henderson estate—she is the only heir to the estate—when she was arrested.

In appearance and at first sight, Clarkton is a sleepy and somewhat undistinguished southern town. However, the arrest of Professor Goodman under the new state law has turned the town into a place of heated contention and anger—on both sides of the issue: although it must be said that the vast majority of the townspeople have no question about her guilt. Yet even

among that group are those who question the death penalty—
particularly since this is one of the very few states that execute
convicted murderers by lethal injection.

Professor Goodman, who is forty-one years old, has two
children, a girl and a boy. Hope, eighteen years old, has just
finished her freshman year at Brown, and the Goodman son,
Leon, has completed his junior year at Harvard. Both children
are traveling in Europe with a university tour group.

According to Millicent Woolton, Professor Goodman is
guilty of no crime, no infraction of the law—indeed nothing that
deserves a prison sentence, much less the death penalty—a punishment that Ms. Woolton calls both barbaric and inhuman.

Three days ago, on the occasion of Professor Goodman's
arrest, Charles Anderson, the district attorney, demanded that
since this was a capital offense in a state where premeditated
murder was punishable by lethal injection, any and all bail
should be denied. Judge Benson then asked Mr. Anderson how
much bail he would ask for if the judge decided to grant bail,
and Mr. Anderson replied that he would ask for a million dollars. According to the record, Judge Benson's reply was as
follows:

"Mr. Anderson, if I set bail at one million dollars, the Goodmans will not have a bit of trouble raising it. Face the fact that
we are juggling a very hot potato here, and don't be fooled by
this moment of quiet. Word has just gotten out, and from here
on in a lot of people are going to make a lot of noise. I want this
to be by the book. We are dealing with a woman who is not only
a college professor, but the last of a fine old family. In the past

few hours, I've been on the phone with the governor twice. This is his baby, and he wants it clean and by the book. I've also been called by the Republican majority leader in the State House, and he's as nervous as a wet hen, and he's been trying to buy himself some comment from the White House. So far, nothing, and if I'm guessing right, it will continue to be nothing. Right here is where the ball goes down. Yesterday we were a sleepy backwater town. Today we're the hub of the universe. So I am going to grant bail. I am going to release Professor Goodman on her own recognizance. That's my judgment. I don't think the lady's going to run."

A middle-aged man with a white mustache introduced himself as the courtroom constable. He wore a gray uniform, and his soft southern speech was totally ingratiating. "My name is Lemuel Southerby, and I'm constable here." The name and the designation made Abigail smile, her first smile that morning.

"You'll be sitting right here," Southerby went on. "I'll have a pitcher of ice water for you and your party, and I'll tend to it through the day. This is a well-built old building, so they never felt no need to air-condition it."

He pointed upward. A line of ceiling fans was turning slowly. "They do more than you might imagine," Southerby said. "Clerk's name is Hoby Schmidt. Stenographer is Sarahbelle.

Nobody bothers to call her anything else, so her family name don't matter." He nodded and returned to his position by the back entrance. A black man in a somber black suit and white shirt dusted the judge's desk delicately with a handkerchief. Then he poured a glass of water.

Abigail noticed that the press table was full, the twelve seats around the table taken, while four still photographers sat cross-legged under the table and in front of it. The seats for the public were filling up, people crowding for a place and being held to order by two policemen. Three men had now taken their place at the prosecution table, and Jack Ridley explained to Abigail: "The chubby one with the blond hair and the gold glasses—that's Charley Anderson, local DA. He's a political animal and wants the governorship, so he's in this for blood. He looks like a mild little bank clerk, but he has the soul and compassion of a hog." Another man brought a small file, which he deposited next to the prosecution table. "Mike Sutter—he's Anderson's gofer, nasty brute. He works for the office, so he's entitled to a badge and a gun. He's an ADA, but this is Anderson's moment of glory, and he'll hog it all."

Jack Ridley said to Bill, "Anderson's not smart. He's dangerous because everyone underestimates him, but he's not smart, and he's not good with Benson. He grew up down by the river, and while I hate to use the word, he's poor white trash."

"That won't mean a damn thing to Benson," Button said. "You know that."

The clerk leaped to his feet now and called out, "All rise. All those having business before this court, please rise!"

Benson entered and took his place behind his desk on the podium.

"Be seated," the clerk said. "The Honorable Judge George Lee Benson presiding."

A ripple of voices, and Benson tapped his gavel for silence. "Ladies and gentlemen," he said, "this is an unusual occasion, and I see in my courtroom a number of faces at the press table that are unfamiliar to me. For them, then, I will state a few rules. No photographs are to be taken in this courtroom, so those photographers who have taken a position in here will please rise and leave. Whatever emotion is expressed here, there is to be no applause or cries of derision. Thank you." And then to the clerk, "Mr. Schmidt, would you please read the indictment."

As the photographers filed out of the courtroom, the clerk rose and read: "The defendant, Abigail Goodman, whose residence is in the town of Hilden, is hereby charged with the violation of section 156 and section 157 in the criminal code of this state."

Then, savoring his position at the apex of the world's attention, so to speak, he read the rest of the indictment much as a high school student might declaim the Gettysburg Address, lingering upon the motive words as if to increase their threat and potency.

Abigail, knowing the indictment only too well, let her attention drift from person to person. Did she read a shadow of distaste on the face of the Judge George Lee Benson? Part of the press scribbled madly, but others picked up the indictment on their small tape recorders, meanwhile studying the audience and officers of the court, even as Abigail was doing—except that Abigail sought clues on the faces of the press. Were they with her? Did they feel or sense anything of her terror?

The clerk finished his reading.

A ripple of sound went across the courtroom. Benson tapped with his gavel for silence and said to the prosecutor, "Mr. Anderson, have you evidence to show cause why Mrs. Goodman should be found in violation of sections 156 and 157?"

Anderson rose and said, "Your Honor, I have here faxed copies of the records of Hilden Hospital, showing that Abigail Goodman was admitted to the hospital on the ninth of May, that is thirty-four days ago. I offer these records as the firm basis for the indictment, according to the laws and rulings of the criminal code of this sovereign state. I offer them now as a statement of proof, and I ask that they also be entered as evidence." Anderson then laid the documents on the judge's desk.

Benson studied the pages in silence for a few minutes, then asked, "How does your client plead, Mr. Ridley?"

"Not guilty, Your Honor."

"You may make your motions now, Mr. Ridley."

"I move that the indictment be voided and rendered invalid," Ridley said.

"On what grounds, Mr. Ridley?"

"In both cases, that is sections 156 and 157, the stipulated punishment violates the constitutional guarantee against cruel and unusual punishment. The governor of this state signed the bill that spells out the laws in question less than forty-eight hours ago, and while the constitution of this state says that a law can be operative from the moment of its passage by the legislature if not vetoed by the governor, the practice is so contrary to the common procedure anywhere else in the country and in the federal government as well, that I hold it cannot be sustained; and finally, the alleged action of which my client is accused is not an act of murder and is not regarded as a criminal action by the legal fraternity the world over. Let me add that while my client knew that the bill in question, namely the addition of sections 156 and 157 to the criminal code, had been passed by the legislature, she and thousands of others accepted the governor's statement that he would veto such a bill. This must be taken into consideration."

Jack Ridley finished and seated himself. Bill tightened his grip on Abigail's hand. Benson turned to Anderson.

"I will rest on the indictment, Your Honor," Anderson said.

"I am going to retire now," the judge stated, "and give Mr. Ridley's motions my attention. Court will convene again at two o'clock. Court is now adjourned."

"To what end?" Abigail wondered. "Is there any chance in the world that he'll throw out the indictment?"

Bill shrugged. "There's always a chance, wouldn't you say?" he asked of Jack Ridley.

"The point is," Button Ridley said to Abigail, "that we have a court, and if we go to trial, we'll have a jury, and already the whole world is watching. It's not Germany and it's not Russia."

"Then what is it?"

"It's our cherished lunacy," Jack said, "and the real problem that faces us now is to get out of here through the mob outside and find some place where we can eat."

"No statements, no remarks," Bill told Abigail, clearing a path for her as he elbowed their way through the crowd. "They have to let us through peacefully."

"They'll learn," Jack told him as they broke loose. "The last time we had this kind of thing was twenty-seven years ago, the last Klan lynching in this town. They put seven of them on trial."

"Were they convicted?" Abigail asked.

"No way. But that was twenty-seven years ago, and Judge Benson was not on the bench."

Abigail could not touch food. The few bites of sandwiches that the others took were chewed grimly and eaten without pleasure. They were back in the courthouse at ten minutes before two. At two precisely, Judge Benson took his seat on the bench. He wasted no time but plunged into the matter.

"I am throwing out the first count of the indictment, section 156 of the criminal code. It is too loosely written to accept it. It makes no mention of age, nor does it deal with conditions at the time of the act of which the defendant is accused. It is written so poorly that it can have no meaning in any court of these United States."

Anderson was on his feet.

"Mr. Anderson?"

"I want an objection put in the record."

"So ordered."

Anderson sank back onto his seat.

"As for the motions put forward by the defense," the judge went on, "I find no validity in them, and they are rejected. The indictment under the violation of section 157 of the criminal code of this state holds, and Abigail Goodman must stand trial. Both the prosecution and the defense are instructed to appear in this courtroom two weeks from today to begin the selection of the jury."

He had hardly finished speaking when Jack Ridley was on his feet, pleading for a continuance. "This is a major trial, Your Honor, on a point never before decided in an American court. My client is on trial for her life, and she and her husband are miles from home and from their records. Give us at least four weeks for preparation."

"Your request is rejected," Benson said coldly, and then he rose and left the bench.

Later that day, discussing what happened, Button Ridley said, "From all I can figure out, on the rumors going around, the governor laid it on the line with Benson. Two weeks and not a day more. They are already beginning to see a hornets' nest, and they want to get it out and over with as soon as possible."

"Not from what I know of Benson," Ridley objected. "I can find no bias in his record. I've been racking my own brain to try to understand why he won't give us more than two weeks, and the only answer I can come up with is no better than a wild guess."

"Go ahead," Button told her husband. "Tell us."

"I know Benson," Ridley said, "Not that we're friends or anything of that sort, but I've tried cases in front of him, and he's
a lawyer, a damn good lawyer, and an absolutely pedantic and
unbiased judge. To see him on the bench in this case is astonishing. Why did he accept it? Well, I can give you one reason to
begin with—he didn't want it to be tried by any of a dozen judges
I can name who'd sell their mothers if the price were right."

"Then why did they choose him?" Bill asked.

"That answers easily enough—because he's beyond suspicion.
A conviction in his court stands up better. The only way I can
see it, they told him that either he starts the trial in two weeks,
or they replace him. Maybe the governor put that to him directly, or maybe he heard it through the grapevine. I'm saying
this because no other explanation fits the case." Now he turned
to his wife. "Well?"

"It makes a sort of sense," Button agreed. "But, Jack, he's a
Republican. They've taken on the Right to Life bunch, heart
and soul. He's human and he has political ambitions."

"Mainly, he's human," Ridley said.

"Anyway," Abigail said, "it's a ray of hope. But he was surely
a cold fish when he turned down the motions."

"He had to," Bill said. "And if Jack's thinking is right, he
would have to knock out Jack's motions without a shred of
sympathy."

"And he did wipe the floor with 156," Button said. "He could
have let it stand. In any case, my friends, we have no choice. We
do it in two weeks or not at all."

June 11. Eileen Mott, special to the *New York Globe:*

So far, under the tutelage of Millicent Woolton, Abigail Goodman has refused any interviews. We have been promised a formal press conference tomorrow. Ms. Woolton, in charge of public relations, a volunteer and one of the pillars of Planned Parenthood in the state of Connecticut, has put together a register of reporters covering the Goodman trial. So far, there are forty-three reporters in Clarkton, representing the United States and eleven other countries. While what follows cannot be considered an interview, I did encounter Abigail Goodman in the restroom. The public restroom was occupied, and as my need was great, a court attendant ushered me into the private restroom, at one side of the court and usually reserved for trial participants. Professor Goodman was ready to leave as I entered, but I begged her for a single question.

Professor Goodman is a tall woman, five feet eight inches, I would guess. Her pictures lose her color. She has ash blond hair streaked with white, gray eyes, good color, and she wears no makeup to speak of. She is attractive, handsome rather than pretty, with strong features. She reveals a pleasant smile when she chooses. That is not often. Her hair is gathered into a bun at the back of her head. She was wearing a suit of blue linen over a white blouse, low heels, and no jewelry apart from her wedding ring, a gold band without stones.

My question was: "What do you think your chances are, Professor Goodman?"

At first I thought she'd simply walk by me, but then she noticed my press card pinned on my dress, paused and smiled, and said, "I like the *Globe*. I read it when I'm in New York. You're asking me what I think my chances are?"

"Please."

"Well, my dear, what can I say? I was born into a simple world. The sun shone during the day and the stars glistened at night. Now I am being charged with the murder of a child that never was. When two and two no longer make four, you can't calculate chances or anything else, can you?"

It began improbably, suddenly. Sometimes a life is torn to pieces slowly, over a time of months or years. She had friends whose lives were like that, disintegrating day by day, torn to shreds in ongoing squabbles and consuming hatreds; and then there were the Claybornes, who lived two houses away from Abigail, and they were like a *Reader's Digest* concoction, both of them handsome, he with a first-rate job, she content to raise three towheaded children, and everyone said weren't the Claybornes wonderful, and wished they were like them—and then their car was hit head on by an out-of-control truck, and the children and the wife died, and the husband was left a paraplegic.

Not as terrible as that. Abigail told herself; nothing was as terrible as that—yet—

It was a warm, gentle spring day.

Bill had driven back to Hilden, where he had a case pending, and Abigail had remained in Clarkton, waiting an extra day for the final papers on the property sale. Bill had no love for Clarkton. Since he was not a southerner, born and bred, what Abigail saw as nuances that could be explained and understood historically were to him suspicions and hypocrisies. He preferred driving a few hundred miles to another few days in Clarkton, and Abigail assured him that she would remain only another day or two and would fly back and join him in Hilden. Bill also had a feeling that she wanted to be alone for a while, with only her memories.

She was in Jack Ridley's office, signing whatever documents were left for her to sign, and it was three o'clock in the afternoon, a warm, hazy afternoon. Jack said to her, "Let's take a walk, Abigail, and talk a little."

Button had left the office.

"Walk? Where?"

"Your choice. Down Henderson Lane?"

"Down memory lane? And then I become stupidly sentimental? Jack, I'm a middle-aged woman."

"I'm not making a pass. I gave up on that. You know I did. I'm very serious today."

"Yes, that'll be the day. All right, we'll walk."

They walked slowly down Cranberry Street toward the river.

Abigail could remember her delight in the names of the streets in that part of town, Cranberry Street, Peach Street, Plum Street, and then Apple Lane. When she was a little girl, she had made a song out of the names:

> *Peach Street, Peach Street,*
> *It's really out of reach street,*
> *But if it should start to rain,*
> *I'll just turn off to Apple Lane.*

She sang it softly. "I was twelve then," she said to Jack.

"I wish I had known you then."

"That would have been nice."

"You were a Henderson," Jack reminded her. "My father worked at the mill. You're still a Henderson."

"Jack!" she said sharply.

"All right, forgive me. This was a rotten morning." He stopped walking and drew her around to face him.

Seeing his face, she asked in alarm, "Jack, what is it? What happened?"

"God help me," he said softly. "I don't know any easy way to tell you this. You're going to be arrested."

"What! What on earth do you mean? Jack, is this some stupid joke?"

"I wish. Indeed I do. You had an abortion up in Hilden."

"How do they know that?"

"That little son of a bitch Charley Anderson swore out a warrant in front of Judge Benson. He was going to send a cop over to arrest you, and I told him I'd break his back if he did, and that I'd surrender you."

"What on God's earth are you talking about?"

Ridley shook his head uneasily, groped for words, and then shook his head again. "I know, I know. There's no easy way. I thought I'd get you outside, just the two of us alone—"

"Jack," she exclaimed, "what are you trying to say? Are you telling me that I am going to be arrested? Why? What for?"

"For murder," he said lamely. "For having an abortion. Because of that idiot law they just passed."

"But everyone knows the governor will veto it."

"Abigail, he didn't veto it. He signed it this morning. They're charging you with murder in the first degree."

She stared at him, as if she saw him for the first time, a big, heavyset man, blue eyes, red hair, his face contorted with sympathy, love, desire. She felt her lips tremble. Suddenly her eyes were wet and she was shaking, and he folded her into his arms. He held her a long moment, and then she pulled away, struggling free.

"Jack, no! For Christ's sake, no!"

"You need me. We need each other."

She had stopped shaking. "Jack, that's no damn good! I'm Bill's wife. That's all. That's it."

"You need me."

"I need a lawyer, not a lover. You want me to go out and find another lawyer. I can. Bill's a lawyer."

"I'm your lawyer, God damn it!"

"All right," she whispered. "We'll go back to your office, and you and Button and I will talk about this."

17

2

June 12. Frank Geller, special to the *Chicago Times:*

The press conference called today by Professor Abigail Goodman took place at the local movie house, the old Loew's Clarkton. Professor Goodman, a fully tenured professor of history at
Hilden College, is the first woman ever to have been arrested
and indicted under the state's new abortion law, which specifies
a charge of murder in the first degree for any woman who con-
sents to an abortion after the first trimester of her pregnancy. The
interest aroused nationally and internationally by her forthcoming trial is attested to by the fact that more than fifty correspondents crowded into the movie house this morning. The press

conference was chaired by Ms. Millicent Woolton, head of publicity for Planned Parenthood in the state of Connecticut, a volunteer to the defense team.

On stage for questioning were the following: Professor Goodman; her husband, William Goodman, an attorney; Jack Ridley, attorney for the defense; and Button Ridley, partner and wife of Jack Ridley. Mr. Goodman is a corporate and tax attorney in Hilden, the Goodmans' hometown. Jack Ridley has a reputation throughout the state as a civil rights attorney. Questions and answers as follows:

Freda Hammond (*The Times*, London): "How does it feel, Professor Goodman, to face a charge of murder for what has never before, in civilized circles, been considered a crime?"

Abigail Goodman: "I think I feel somewhat like Alice in Wonderland, somewhat like in a dream. My tactile sense convinces me that I am here and that all this is happening. My common sense tells me that it is impossible. The trouble is that I cannot cry out, as Alice did, that my accusers are a pack of cards and brush them all away."

Joan Armond (*Le Monde*, Paris): "Professor Goodman, you can imagine the great interest in your travail in France. We have heard a great deal about the phrase in America, 'the war against the women.' Is this a part of the war against the women?"

Abigail Goodman: "Yes. Certainly this is a part of the war against women."

Ranjana Ponta (*Indian Express*, New Delhi): "My question is for Mr. Jack Ridley. I represent an Indian newspaper. We have terrible problems of overpopulation. I know that this is not yet a severe problem in your country, but I hear about thousands of poverty-stricken girls who become pregnant, who are cocaine addicts. Their children could be brain-damaged or born with the AIDS disease. How can this criminal code be justified?"

Jack Ridley: "Our state legislature is elected by the voters. They have the right to make whatever laws they please. If citizens do not like or respect these laws, they can appeal. If Mrs. Goodman should be found guilty in this trial—a result I hardly believe possible—we will appeal. We will appeal to the Supreme Court, if necessary."

Freda Hammond: "But, Mr. Ridley, your Supreme Court has—well, we know what has happened to your Supreme Court. What possible reason might they have to come to Professor Goodman's defense?"

Jack Ridley: "The law, madam. I am a lawyer. I must put my faith in the law and the Constitution."

Wolf Schwartz (*Stern* magazine, Hamburg): "I must address this question to Ms. Goodman. You are a professor of history, are you not?"

Abigail Goodman: "I am, yes."

Wolf Schwartz: "In Germany under Adolf Hitler, certain abortions were punishable by death. Would you agree that the level of a modern democracy can be measured by its attitude toward women—I mean by that the democratic level, do you follow?"

Abigail Goodman: "Yes. An excellent way to measure the level of democracy in any country."

Karl Benski (*Izvestia*, Moscow): "For Mr. Goodman—Mr.

Goodman, I am of the knowledge of your American Constitution, having read it carefully. It prohibits cruel or unusual punishment. Is not a death sentence for an abortion cruel and unusual punishment?"

William Goodman: "It is."

Frank Geller (*Chicago Times*): "For Mr. Ridley—Mr. Ridley, if your client has violated section 157 of the criminal code, has she or has she not participated in a murder?"

Jack Ridley: "The answer is absolutely not."

Eileen Mott (*New York Globe*): "Question for Button Ridley—I have heard that eminent counsel, both American and European, have offered their services on a pro bono basis. You and your husband constitute a small legal firm. Have you thought of enlarging your defense team?"

Button Ridley: "We have discussed this point, and we certainly may ask eminent counsel to join us at some time in the future. But my husband and I have practiced civil rights law here for the past two decades. We feel that we know the courts and understand the people. So for the time being, we are preparing our case with the help of the Goodmans, of course."

Conte Laponi (*Avante,* Rome): "Professor Goodman, I have heard rumors that both the pope and the archbishop of Canterbury have been approached to intercede. Is there any truth in this?"

Abigail Goodman: "It's the first I've heard of it."

"Would you approve if it were so?"

Abigail Goodman: "I have no desire to be executed. We will welcome help from anywhere."

"What about plea bargaining? Have you made any attempt to strike a deal?"

Abigail Goodman: "Sir, there is no deal to be made, and I will not plead guilty to any lesser charge. I believe wholly that the abortion issue is being used, and indeed the Right to Life movement is being used, to drive women back into their condition of a hundred years ago. I don't for a moment believe that the collection of corrupt and inept men who make up our legislature and have put this law into effect give a tinker's damn about abortion or the question of when the embryo becomes a person before the law. They are engaged in a war against women, and this is their tool and their weapon."

This ended the questioning, and there is some feeling on the part of this correspondent (Frank Geller, *Chicago Times*) that the lawyers functioning in Professor Goodman's defense were somewhat taken aback by her outburst. There were some remarks to the effect of it being the wrong place for a closing statement. On the other hand, there was a good deal of applause from the press.

"Of course I was impressed," Abigail told Bill. "I'm not sophisticated enough to brush it off. My word, Bill, these are the lineal descendents of Pallas Athene, and in a country where a semiliterate actor can become president, stars are worshiped. I don't know whether it helps, but I'm not cynical at this point. I'm damn grateful they decided to fly down."

Every reporter was scribbling their words. "We stand with you!" declared the tall, lovely redhead. There were three of them, and, as the *L.A. Times* pointed out the following day, their combined salaries for their most recent films, three films, amounted to twenty-two million dollars. Barbra, who had refused to sing in her last five films, now sang *The House I Live In*. She had never sung it before. The stringer for the *Hollywood Reporter* wrote, "That golden voice made the golden afternoon in this once sleepy southern town." The third star, a tall, slender black-haired woman, spoke as the voice of the Screen Actors Guild, "To you, Abigail, we pledge our voice, our strength, and all the love of the sisterhood of women." They stood on the steps of the courthouse, the center of a mass of television cameras, reporters, cameramen, and at least a third of the town's population.

Anderson, the district attorney, told Jim Horst, the police chief, that he had to break it up—to which Horst snorted that something like this, which had never happened before and would likely never happen again, was not something he intended to break up, especially since his wife was there in the crowd, right up front by virtue of her political position.

It was wonderful, Abigail felt, to be embraced by the three film stars and to be taken into their emotion and tears and fervent pledges of support; but by nightfall they were gone in the private plane they had hired.

23

"It was like a movie for a little while," she told Bill. "Then it stopped being like a movie."

June 13. Julia Hyde, City Press Syndicate:

Today, eleven busloads of women descended upon Clarkton, carrying placards and banners of the National Organization for Women. They formed a picket line in front of the courthouse, and they announced to the assembled press that this picket line would be renewed and enlarged as long as the trial lasted. Gathering together in the square opposite the courthouse, they were addressed by Freda Swanson, the director of Connecticut Planned Parenthood. Ms. Swanson, a tall, striking woman of fifty, white-haired and commanding, called out:

"My friends, sisters in our age-long struggle, this hallowed spot has been chosen as Armageddon. It is hallowed because here we will win the right to exist as free citizens of this country. It is Armageddon because the forces of light are here arrayed against the forces of evil!"

"The forces of evil," in the shape of a couple of dozen jeering, shouting, and swearing white men, appeared almost by magic. They used every profanity they knew, and finally they were faced by Freda Swanson, who informed their leader that while the women were nonviolent, there were limits, whereupon she swung her handbag and sent the man staggering back on his heels. This resulted in what came to be known as the "animal attack," men on women, and the six policemen assigned to the meeting did not interfere until they realized that the enraged women, falling back at first before the men, had turned on them with handbags, canes, and umbrellas.

The men—in fact there were twenty-two of them, as near as anybody could make a count—had little or no opinions on abortion but were, according to the local police, rednecks out of work or just plain bums who never worked if they could help it. As one of the men put it, it turned their stomachs to see a mob of "out-of-town bimbos taking over the place," and they felt they had to do something about it.

It was the reaction on the part of the women that made the occasion unique, if not historic. Presumably the intention of the men was to hoot and jeer and give vent to their hostility and lend amusement to what might otherwise be simply another boring afternoon; but when the insults flung at the women passed the limits of ordinary, indecent profanity, Ms. Freda Swanson of Planned Parenthood of Connecticut swung her purse and hit Jim Constance, an unemployed riverboat worker. He later claimed that the blow from the metal trimming of the purse damaged the sight in his left eye.

The men evidently had no plan of attack and were taken entirely by surprise by the anger of the women. It was as if the whole half century of these women in the practice of nonviolence had suddenly reached the breaking point and exploded. The police assigned to the meeting held back until they realized that the lives of the men actually were endangered. By then, reinforcements had arrived, and every available policeman in Clarkton was on the scene. Eleven of the hecklers had to be hospitalized, none of them with life-threatening injuries. Sixteen women had to be treated for cuts and bruises, none serious enough to require hospitalization. Thirty-one of the women, including Ms. Swanson, were arrested on charges of disturbing the peace.

By late afternoon the women had regrouped, managed to paint several placards, which called for freedom for Freda Swanson and for her sisters in the struggle and respect for their First Amendment rights, and had once more gathered in the town square. This time, five hundred or so of the local citizens gathered to hoot, jeer, applaud, and denounce. Madelin Garcia of San Antonio Choice replaced Freda Swanson at the podium, and when the cops tried to break up the meeting and reach the podium, the women formed a circle, arms linked. The police were remarkably restrained, some of them dwelling on the curious contrast of the incident to its background, the fine old square sitting there in the warm June sunlight, the celebratory and requisite statue of the Confederate soldier, and the Confederate flag along with the Stars and Stripes floating over the bandstand. It finished with the arrest of eleven more women.

The day of the riot in the bandstand square, Jack Ridley presented Charles Anderson with a tentative list of the defense witnesses—and received in return the State's witnesses. William and Abigail Goodman had put together what they regarded as a very solid group for the defense: two physicians, a Congregational minister, an Episcopal bishop, Helen Bradley from the National Organization for Women, an MIT professor, and a jurist who was a national authority on constitutional law.

The prosecution list began with Rabbi Herschel Cohen.

"This is really out of left field," Ridley said.

"But it makes sense," Button said. "They know that Bill's Jewish—everyone in town knows it by now, and they're covering all bases."

"What do you know about Rabbi Herschel Cohen?" Ridley asked. "Have you ever heard of him?"

"Rigid. Orthodox Hasidic—which you could compare to a twice born fundamentalist Baptist who knows beyond question that the world was created in six days, just as the Bible says. They agree on that," Bill said, smiling bitterly. "Abortion? Good God, no, never. He heads up a congregation in New York City, in Brooklyn, and he gets a lot of headlines simply by being against most of what we're for. He will swear on the Bible that abortion is the ultimate sin."

"Find us a rabbi who thinks differently," Button said.

"Rabbi Frank Green from Hilden," Abigail said. "Why didn't we think of him? He's as close to a saint as we'll find in any of the religion fraternity."

"On abortion?" Ridley wanted to know.

"Solid Choice advocate. Speaks at their meetings."

"Then that's it," Button said.

"Is it a wise move?" Bill asked.

"For heaven's sake, Bill," Abigail said, "you can't believe we're going through this without a whisper of anti-Semitism in the air."

Bill spread his arms. "I'm convinced."

"It's all right." She went to him and put an arm around his waist. He had always been her rock, her support, but down here something had happened to him. Physically he was hard; her arm touched nothing soft or fat. He was a big man, and it had always given her comfort to have a big man around. He was gentle; even in court he was not threatening or abrasive. She was beginning to understand how frightened, how absolutely terror-stricken, he was—and with that the degree to which he adored her, treasured her. When he covered his fear, he withdrew and made a shell around him.

She had put the question of Jewishness to him at the beginning of their entrapment. "I know there's a Jewish community here," she told him. "I remember it from the summers here when I was a kid. It's an old antebellum mansion they bought for a synagogue soon after the Civil War. They keep a low profile, but they have property and wealth, and they're not without influence."

Bill had refused to go to them, to ask anything in the way of help from them. He pointed out to her that he was Jewish by birth and she was not. Whatever the Jewish community in Clarkton was, it had not come to him; it would be a mockery for him to turn to them. "They'll see it as endangering them. I can't blame them, but I couldn't bear to go there and be turned away."

Abigail waited until she was alone in Jack Ridley's office before she put through a call to Rabbi Frank Green. A few minutes before this, Bill had received a call from a Mr. Hogan, who said he was conducting the wrecking of the old Henderson house, and there were some things that Mr. Goodman might want to look at before all the junk was hauled away. Bill left to go to the old house, and Abigail called Hilden.

"Abigail," the rabbi said, "I've been thinking of you these past few days, and praying. How are you bearing up under all this lunacy?"

"I'm not sure of anything."

"And Bill?"

"It's harder on Bill."

"Yes, I can understand that. What can I do to help?"

"Frank," Abigail said, "I'm turning to you because you're an old friend and I know how you feel about the rights of women. The prosecution is putting on a witness, Rabbi Herschel Cohen."

"So that's it."

"You know him?"

"Who doesn't? He'll find more photo opportunities than the president. He's a nasty old reprobate, but then I speak as a Reform Jew. His followers consider him the holiest thing since the prophet Elizer. But death for abortion? No, he'll never support that, and there's nothing in the religion to support it."

"Frank, if they're calling him as a witness, doesn't that mean he'll be on their side?"

"No, it only means they want a rabbi as one of their witnesses.

Abigail, are you going to ask me to be a witness for the defense?"

"Yes."

"There's nothing I'd like more, not only to speak for you, but to be there with you and Bill. But I have a record in Clarkton. I was arrested there during the civil rights struggles of the sixties, not only for trying to march through town with a contingent of clergymen, black and otherwise, but a second time after we were released for trying to integrate a restaurant, in the course of which, being much younger, I broke my pledge of nonviolence and punched out a counterman. Six of us served three months in Clarkton. Can you imagine what an attorney would make of me on the witness stand?"

"Yes, I can," Abigail said. "Can you suggest someone else?"

"It would be a mistake. Let Cohen speak his piece. It might bounce right back at them. I have a friend here, Sister Jean O'Malley, a Maryknoll nun, who has just returned from two years in India, mostly in Bangladesh, and will make a much more impressive witness than I would."

"A Catholic?"

"Exactly."

"But how can she? We've tried desperately to find a priest. We talked to priests who will protest the death sentence but will not support abortion under oath. What makes Sister O'Malley different?"

"Guts, faith. We've spoken about this awful trial. Let me talk to her."

Abigail put down the telephone, leaned back, and tried to

calm herself, to put her feelings together and find a center for herself. She had slept poorly the night before. Now, closing her eyes, she found herself dozing, drifting away, back to this place in her childhood, a small girl in the attic of Grandma Henderson's house coming on an old leather trunk and having the temerity to open it, but very quietly. It was packed full of clothes, wonderful, ancient clothes. She put on a dress of marvelous lace and ruffles. She struggled to get into boots that came up to her thighs. All that summer she made visits to the attic, never sure whether her grandmother knew about it or not. But when she climbed up to the attic the following summer, the old leather trunk was gone. She burst into tears when her grandfather told her he had given it to a museum in Washington. She was ready to burst out with, "But it was mine! How could you! How could you give it away!"

Button came into the room and announced lunch. "Salad this time. I made it at home, crawfish and local lettuce and greens, southern food—where's Bill?"

"Something about the people who are tearing down the house."

"Abby, I drove by there yesterday. Not a stick left of it. They were dragging and smoothing the land for paving."

"Then why—"

The telephone rang. Jack Ridley answered and handed it to Abigail. It was Bill. "Abby," he said, his voice strained and hoarse, "I don't want you to get upset."

"Bill, what happened? Where are you?"

"I'm in the County Hospital. I'm not hurt—just bumps and

bruises. But our car is finished. Get Jack to drive you over here."

A few minutes later, Abigail and Jack pulled up at the County Hospital, an old red-brick structure that had been the county armory before the Civil War and had been rescued from ruin, rebuilt, and turned into a hospital some fifty years ago. Bill was waiting for them in the lobby. He had three gauze patches on his face—on his chin, cheek, and his forehead. A lump on his head. His suit was torn and dirty, the seersucker stained with blood, and as Abigail and Ridley entered the hospital he pulled himself out of his chair and said bluntly, "Let's get the hell out of here."

"What happened?"

"Just get me out of here first."

Abigail kissed him gently.

"Bastards," Bill said. "Redneck bastards."

June 14. Frank Geller, special to the *Chicago Times:*

Mayor Herbert Holmby of Clarkton agreed today to grant this correspondent the first one-on-one interview since the arrest of Abigail Goodman. Until now, as Mayor Holmby informed me, his purpose had been to keep a consistently low profile and to separate himself from the case, devoting himself entirely to the function of the community and the maintenance of, as he put it, a decent level of law and order in the community. The hysterical mob scene, presented by outsider groups of pro-abortion women the previous day, persuaded him to change his mind.

Mayor Holmby had just pleaded with Judge Benson for an injunction against further demonstrations. Judge Benson had been loath to grant such an injunction, stating that for the good of the case and the State's position, further infringements on the First Amendment and the Constitution should be resisted.

I immediately asked Mayor Holmby whether he considered Criminal Statute 157 to be an infringement on the First Amendment. He replied that he did not.

"Are you going to get the injunction?" I asked him.

"No, I am not," the mayor replied.

Mayor Holmby then stated that Mr. Goodman and the crew—his word—around Jack Ridley were responsible for the outbreak of lawlessness on the part of the out-of-state women. "Do you realize, sir, that I have forty-two women in jail? We don't have forty-two cells in Clarkton. A crook has a right to one of our cells. A woman does not, especially a Yankee woman. And do you know what she says, this Swanson woman? She says that they can bring ten thousand more down here, and the more we arrest the more will come to take their place. What in God's name are you going to do about it? How do we feed them? Where is the money coming from?"

"Do you wish to be quoted on this?" I asked the mayor.

"Absolutely," he replied.

"What do you intend to do with the forty-two women you have arrested?" I asked him.

"I suppose we'll release them, maybe fine them fifty dollars each. We can use the money. Good heavens, we're not a rich town. We had a wagon works here, the last real wagon works in these United States—made wagons for Europe and Asia, ceremonial stuff. They once had an order for three hundred wagons from the Soviet Union, when there was a Soviet Union. Made wagons for Hollywood films. Well, it closed down and put two hundred twenty people out of work. That's why they got so riled at that cotton-picking lot of harridans from up north."

I assured him that there were thousands of Right to Life women in the North, and that he'd find them coming down to speak their piece.

"Yes, speak their piece, but peacefully. Get it, young feller?"

I asked him when the women would be released.

"Just as soon as possible. They may be wild liberals or something, but they got appetites like healthy young mares. It's going to cost us two hundred dollars a day to feed them. I just wish to damnation they'd go on one of them hunger strikes."

3

June 15. Ranjana Ponta, the *Indian Express:*

There are so many peculiarities attached to this case, so many contradictions, that it becomes almost impossible to explain to Indian readers exactly what is happening. We have so long revered the United States as a land of unlimited freedom, that this trial of a woman, facing a death penalty for undergoing an abortion, would appear to be a total contradiction of everything the United States stands for. However, the anti-abortion movement reconciles its limitations of personal freedom with the proposition that the embryo in the womb is a person entitled to human rights.

In carrying out its campaign against abortion, the movement has shown small evidence of generosity toward adults and has on occasion engaged in violence. Here in the town of Clarkton, there have been indications of violence from the day Professor Goodman was indicted. Not only did an overt attack take place against a large delegation of women who had been bussed in to protest the indictment, but Professor Goodman's husband, William Goodman, who is participating as part of the defense, has been subject to physical abuse and anti-Semitism.

Lured to a spot on the outskirts of Clarkton, where Professor Goodman's family once owned property (their original appearance in Clarkton was to dispose of that property), Mr. Goodman was set upon by a gang of hoodlums, screaming anti-Semitic slanders. He was badly beaten. While he did not have to be hospitalized, several stitches were taken in his scalp.

There was a time, not too many years ago, when black people in the Clarkton area were as shabbily treated as the blacks in South Africa or the untouchables here in India. While much of this has changed, due to the civil rights movement of the 1960s, there are evidences that racial antagonism is increasing. Since the need for public funding of abortion is greatest among the poor—particularly blacks—and since the Right to Life movement, the anti-abortion movement, is practically all middle-class white, it is understandable that it could coincide with the increasing racism in America.

"I was scared to death," Bill admitted. "I thought they were going to kill me. I didn't think about it. I just struck out like a damn fool. Then I was hit on the head with something, knocked over, and kicked in the face. Someone doused my car with gasoline. I saw that out of the corner of my eye. They lit the gas, and the sheet of flame distracted them, and I stumbled to my feet and ran like hell toward the steamroller. I got behind it before the car exploded, and two of the men raced off and must have driven away. I think they had parked at the other end of the tarmac. Then the fire engines and an ambulance came, and they patched me up at the hospital."

"Thank God you're all right," Abigail said.

"What about the men working on the tarmac?" Ridley asked. "They saw it?"

"They watched and never did a damn thing."

Jim Horst, the police chief, was waiting for them at Ridley's office. "How are you, Goodman?" he asked Bill.

"I'm still alive."

"Sorry this had to happen on my turf. We got hoodlums and bums. Tell me who hasn't. We picked up two of them."

"Who are they?" Jack demanded. "I sure as hell want to know who paid for this."

"Jack, don't start driving me crazy with conspiracy theories.

The ones we're holding are a couple of bums who hang out down by the river. It's the third one who worries me. When Goodman here hit him, he broke his jaw and knocked him out, and then he got burned when the car went up. If he dies, we'll be in a fix."

"He held a gun on me," Bill said coldly.

"We didn't find no gun."

"They came to beat him up and burn his car. No bum reaches into his pocket to buy a can of gasoline to burn up the car of somebody he doesn't know," Jack Ridley said. "Not with gasoline at a dollar seventy a gallon, because when a bum like that has a dollar and seventy cents in his pocket, he spends it on rotgut. So don't threaten us and don't try to make this stink any more than it does."

"Getting tough, Jack? That's not your style," the chief said. "Don't push me. Nobody invited the Goodmans down here. They just turned up at this poor, backward southern town to make a buck selling Grandma's house—and a pretty big buck, too. You squeezed the juice out of Buddy Johnson with the price you put on that old wreck of Henderson's. What the hell— the mall's good for the town."

"*Mal de mall,*" Bill said bitterly. Ridley burst out laughing.

"What the hell does that mean?" the chief wanted to know. "Why don't you let me in on the joke? It might be the last good laugh in this case."

"He's a sweetheart," Abigail said after Horst had left.

"Oh, yes," Button agreed. "We turn them out down here, like Central Casting. *Mal de mall,*" she said to Bill. "I like that."

Bill smiled painfully.

"Bill, they could have killed you," Abigail said. "What is happening here? They wanted to kill you."

"Maybe not," Jack said, putting his arm around Abigail's shoulder—the first time he had made such a gesture since the case began.

Afterward, alone with her husband, Button said, "Don't start anything, Jack."

"What's that supposed to mean?"

"You know what it means. For once in your life, try to understand what it means to be a woman. You must look at Abigail only as a client. That's what she is, a client—only a client, a sensible, smart woman, but a client and not something to be conquered. She is not part of the marketplace."

"That stinks!" Ridley snorted.

"You still don't know what's happening here," his wife said. "It's not abortion, it's women—it's the war against women that has been going on since history began—and this woman, Abigail Goodman, is chosen for slaughter. Try to understand that—that's all I'm asking."

At eight o'clock that evening, the Ridleys and the Goodmans, still in the office, still working, heard a hoot of victory as Jim Cooper, a law student working for the Ridleys, burst into the place. "Good news and bad news!" he shouted.

"Calm down," Button said.

"Calm down? Me? No way. You know the Purple Shade?"

"Poolroom and bar—edge of town, mostly black," Ridley said.

"Right. Well, I've been poking around there. That's one advantage of being black. You can move in on a place like that,
and it takes a little longer before they close up and throw you
out. Only they didn't close up on me, because when I told them
I'm working for you folks, they sort of liked that, and when I
whispered some names of the State's witnesses and mentioned
the Reverend Jason Homer, a couple of them just broke up and
laughed fit to bust a gut. You want to know why? I'll be just
delighted to tell all you white folks why."

"Jim Cooper," Button said, "enough! What have you got?"

"Well, there is one of these nasty, tough operators, and he just
loves the way I talk fancy white talk, and someday I'll be a big
lawyer and keep him out of the cooler. His name is Baron Omi,
spelled O-m-i, but pronounced Oh-my, and he has this sweet
little lassie named Sweet Sue, and I saw her and she is one lovely
fox, not exactly a hooker, but she turns tricks when it takes her
fancy, and Omi is her pimp, more or less, but decent if you can
think that way about a pimp. So when this white feller goes
absolutely crazy about Sweet Sue, Omi lays off, and he doesn't
see Sweet Sue for five, six weeks, and she gives it only to this
white feller, and sure as such things happen, she finds herself
with child, as they say. So she decides to have an abortion, and
this white man agrees with her and gives her one thousand
dollars to go to a hospital way up in Ohio and have her abortion
there. And she does. And Omi is laughing himself into a hernia
because the name of the white man"—he paused and let them
hang on his words—"is none other than number two on the
State's list of witnesses, the Reverend Jason Homer."

He sat down, folded his hands in his lap, and faced them, a slight smile on his face.

"How do you know he was telling you the truth?" Ridley demanded.

"He didn't know that the State would call Homer as a witness, but he knows about Homer's crusade against abortion. Anyway, nobody invents a story like that."

"Where was the abortion?"

"The Canbury Clinic in Cleveland."

"All right. Get on a plane tomorrow and talk to them."

"They won't give anything."

"Try. Meanwhile, will Sweet Sue testify?"

"If Omi says so, and he'll make his price reasonable."

"I think we finally have something," Bill said.

"Maybe," Button told them, "maybe not. If one of the reverend's parishioners is on the jury, it might backfire. We'll have to think about it."

But later that night, Abigail said to Bill, "What happens to Reverend Homer? This just about finishes everything for him, doesn't it?"

"We can't worry about that. Damn these people, why can't they live decently with their sins and not pull the whole human race into it?"

July 1. Eileen Mott, special to the *New York Globe:*

Today, in this once-quiet southern town that has now become world famous, the selection of a jury for the Abigail Goodman trial begins. Ironically, Clarkton is a town where Professor Goodman's family has been an important presence for the past two hundred years. Her grandmother, Martha Henderson, the last Henderson living in Clarkton, died only months ago. Professor Goodman and her husband were in town, arranging for the disposal of Martha Henderson's home, when Professor Goodman was arrested. The family house has since been torn down, the area covered with tarmac to create a shopping center.

Professor Goodman has stated that she has every confidence in the integrity and sense of fairness of the townspeople, regardless of whom is chosen for the jury. Together with Maybel Rizel of the *San Francisco Inquirer,* I engaged in a poll of 100 townspeople, 50 men, 50 women, 20 percent black. Of the 40 white men, 29 said they would vote a guilty verdict, 5 were undecided, and 6 felt that she was unjustly charged. Of the white women, 17 refused to answer any questions, 26 supported a guilty verdict, and 14 were for Professor Goodman. Out of 10 black men, 6 claimed no opinion and 4 voted innocent. Out of 10 black women, 9 were for acquittal and only 1 for conviction. All of the blacks and most of the whites either refused to give their names or obtained a promise from us not to print any names.

Jim Cooper, the black law student who is part of the Ridley-Goodman defense team, says that such off-the-cuff opinions mean little, that southerners regard questions from the northern press with suspicion and some hostility.

"Good morning, Miss Abigail," the constable said. He led her to the defense table. The others, Bill and Jack and Button Ridley and Jim Cooper, joined them, Cooper still glowing with his discovery, via Baron Omi, even though he had found absolutely nothing in Cleveland in the way of evidence. Bill remained hopeful about Jim's discovery, but Jack pointed out that this was not one of those southern towns with a black police chief, and indeed there was no town in this state that had a black police chief, and that all in all it was a pretty benighted place. "And Jim's story," Jack said, "rests on Sweet Sue as a witness."

"She's agreed, hasn't she?"

"Wait until we give her name to Charley Anderson."

"Can you hold off until the last moment?" Abigail asked.

"That depends. The judge may instruct that he wants no surprise witnesses," Jack said. "With Benson you simply don't know what he will do. On the other hand, if we spring Sweet Sue as a surprise witness and the judge finds out that we had her stashed all along, he is not going to be happy. And you can be sure he will find out. Charley Anderson's a bastard, but he's not an idiot. And we can't be sure that she won't run for cover and not testify at all. By now you've realized that Clarkton is no place to extol civil rights."

Bill reassured Abigail, "Anderson will still call Jason Homer as a witness."

"And Sweet Sue?"

Attorneys for both sides were preparing to voir dire the jury, an expression, as Bill explained to Abigail, which meant to plumb for the truth. "Antique," Bill said. "They cling to things down here."

They sat behind the defense table, and nothing happened except that the media were quarreling about the first three rows, which had been set aside for them. It was not enough. They were shy at least fifteen seats. Lemuel Southerby, the constable, was discussing the situation with Eileen Mott, one of two writers the *New York Globe* had dispatched to cover the trial. She was trying to convince Southerby that the *Globe* deserved two seats, since *The Washington Post* and the *Richmond Times* had been granted two seats each.

"Why don't we start?" Abigail asked Bill.

"Not until the clerk calls the judge." Then he added, "Frank called early this morning." Frank Brodsky was Bill's law partner in Hilden.

"He wants to be here?"

"Desperately. I can't let him. Someone has to keep the office going."

Southerby had settled the argument among the reporters by

moving spectators out of half of a fourth row. Every other seat in the courtroom was taken.

"It doesn't matter," Abigail said.

"Of course it matters."

"No, no, it doesn't matter. Nothing can change these people. This is their place, and they are going to damn well execute a woman for having an abortion."

"Abby, Abby, please."

Button gripped her arm. "Abby, we are going to kick the living daylights out of them. I promise you."

Hoby Schmidt, the clerk, rose and chanted, "Everybody rise! Everybody rise! The Honorable Judge George Lee Benson presiding. This court is in session, and God bless the United States of America!"

They stood as Judge Benson entered and took his seat at the bench.

"Be seated," Schmidt said.

Briskly and matter-of-factly, Judge Benson said, "If either the defense or the state has additional motions to make, you may make them now before we begin the selection of the jury."

"The state has no motions to make," Anderson said.

Ridley rose and asked for a change of venue.

"For what reason, Mr. Ridley?"

"On the grounds of prejudice."

"And since you know this state, what makes you think that any other courthouse would bring to bear less prejudice, as you call it?"

Bill had argued against a change of venue with Jack Ridley,

holding that the devil they knew was less dangerous than the devil they did not know. Bill held that from what he could see of the situation, Benson was an asset, their only real asset. Ridley feared Benson's reputation as a strict practitioner. They had just received an offer from the famous criminal lawyer Marcus Steinman, and Bill had reacted initially with some excitement. Ridley brushed it aside coldly, saying that the last thing they needed was a Yankee criminal lawyer—who had agreed to join them on a pro bono basis—and especially one who was Jewish. When Abigail's hackles rose at that, he begged her to understand that he was spelling out what would take place in the jury, not expressing his own feelings.

"Ms. Goodman's relationship to this city," Ridley told the judge.

"But since it could work in the opposite manner, I see no virtue in your request for a change of venue, and I am going to reject the motion."

"Your Honor," Ridley said, "I am also going to move for a continuance, on the grounds that the brutal attack upon my associate, Mr. Goodman, by local thugs robbed us of precious time needed for preparation."

"Mr. Ridley, Mr. Goodman was not incapacitated. No, I see no reason for a continuance."

Bill whispered to Abigail: "I think we're in luck. Benson has already given an appeal court reason enough to void a guilty verdict."

"Lucky," said Abigail, "like the good luck that happens when your house burns down and you're not in it."

"Don't believe it, Bill," Button said. "I wish it were so, but it isn't. They won't void any verdict because he denies us time."

The judge called both lawyers to the bench. "Before we voir dire the jury panel," he told them, "I want to make certain things plain. These are your boundaries. No woman is to be asked whether she has ever had an abortion or approves or disapproves of abortion. No man is to be asked about approval or disapproval. I want an intelligent, balanced jury. They will be brought in from the jury room six at a time."

The first group, three men, three women, seated themselves in the jury box. The clerk called out, "Sherman Hoxbury!"

A large black man, over six feet, heavy and unsmiling, rose and looked about the room.

"Good man," Jim Cooper whispered to Bill. "Works at the power plant. Tight union. Not easy to get him fired. Take him."

Max Quinton, assistant district attorney, pointed to the black man, said, "Peremptory."

"You're dismissed," the clerk said to Hoxbury. "You can go home, sir."

"Hope Williams!" the clerk called.

A pin-faced, round-cheeked woman of about forty rose and nodded.

"Mrs. Williams?" the judge said.

"Sir—Your Honor—how shall I talk to you?"

"As you wish," Benson said. "What is your profession?"

"I'm a housewife."

"And how old are you?"

"Thirty-nine, Your Honor."

"Do you have children?"

"Three," she said, smiling.

"Do you know why Ms. Abigail Goodman is on trial, and what is the nature of the accusation leveled against her?"

"Yes, Your Honor."

"And how do you know?"

"On the telly, the TV, and the *Tribune.*"

"The *Clarkton Tribune,* our local paper?"

"Yes, Your Honor."

"Would you like to serve on this jury, and do you think you can decide this case fairly?"

"Yes, Your Honor."

"Who'll take care of the children?"

"My daughter is sixteen. She can do it."

The judge nodded at Anderson.

Anderson did the questioning himself. He rose and studied Hope Williams thoughtfully. "Are you a churchgoer?" he asked.

"Yes, sir."

"Is your husband alive?"

"Oh, yes."

"And does he live at home?"

"Yes, sir."

"And what does he do for a living, Mrs. Williams?"

"He's chief cashier at State National."

"I accept this juror," Anderson said.

At the defense table, they had been making notes on their yellow pads. Abigail wrote, "I think so." Bill wrote, "She looks honest." Jack wrote, "Husband in bank. No." Button wrote, "Save our peremptories." Jim Cooper wrote, "White folks."

"Mrs. Williams, do you believe in capital punishment?" Jack said.

She hesitated. Then she said, "I don't believe in inflicting pain on others."

"Take her," Button whispered.

"I agree," Abigail said, and Ridley told the court that the juror was acceptable.

"I don't like her," he whispered to Bill, "but there's a point here. We're reasonable and agreeable. The judge will remember that."

But after that, reason and agreement appeared to have departed, and when the court broke for lunch, no second juror had been chosen. The prosecution had used three peremptory challenges, the defense had challenged four people for cause. Two of them were construction workers, one of the two employed on the new mall. One of the construction workers defined himself. He said flatly, pointing to Abigail, "Them bitches are responsible for most of what's wrong with the world today!" The other construction worker had been married and then divorced from a woman who had had an abortion. A nurse who was employed by the Right to Life movement satisfied the judge, as did an elderly lady who had never heard of "such doings" in her time.

At lunch, Millicent Woolton told Abigail that Dede Brown, of National Public Radio, was in town and requested a one-on-one interview. Abigail had been avoiding such interviews, but Millicent stressed this one as important. Both Bill and Ridley agreed.

"This is not only a black woman," Millicent said, "but National Public Radio is unique. It reaches people who think and who do things. I know Dede Brown, and I've heard her stuff."

The afternoon wore on, with the repetitive process of jury selection. There was one moment of excitement, when a tall, austere man, Prayer Phillips by name, identified himself as a messenger of God.

"I asked you what your profession was, sir," Judge Benson said, "not your religion."

"I spoke my profession. I am God's holy messenger."

"You wear your collar backwards. Are you a minister?"

"As Saint Paul was."

Abigail could have sworn that she saw a tiny quiver of Benson's lip, a twinkle in his eye, as if he were saying to himself, Let's put this nut on the jury and do it up right.

But whatever Benson's thoughts were, aloud he said, "I'll entertain a motion for cause."

"So moved," Ridley said.

"You can leave," the judge told the messenger.

"I will not leave. I am here in the name of the Almighty. I will sit in judgment of this whore, this abomination, this daughter of evil—"

The judge had signaled to Southerby and the two policemen who stood at a side aisle, and they descended on the messenger and carried him bodily from the courtroom, while the audience applauded wildly, possibly for the cops or possibly for the messenger.

Benson hammered with his gavel and roared, in an entirely unexpected basso of a voice, "I'll have silence or I'll clear this court! Another such outburst and I will clear it! And keep it cleared!"

The afternoon provided a second juror, Norman Lotts, who gave his profession as a retired policeman.

"Where?" the judge asked him.

"Up north in Boston. But I was born in this state."

"And how long are you retired?"

"Ten years. I'm seventy years old."

"Would you like to sit on this jury?"

"That's what I'm here for."

Anderson accepted without any questions. Bill had scribbled, "Yes, a cop would understand evidence." Button wrote, "No opinion. Got to think. Slow questions." Abigail wrote, "Just maybe—only if he has children." Ridley whispered, "Yeah, if he's childless, he might be carrying a bitter nut."

"I don't like cops," Jim Cooper said.

"You question," Ridley said to Bill.

Bill rose slowly, looking at Lotts with as kindly an expression as he could muster at the moment. Lotts had a lean, almost lipless face. It could mean no teeth, Abigail told herself. She watched Bill as he swallowed and cleared his throat. A prayer went with each juryman. He or she could be my life, my salvation, all my hopes and dreams.

"Are you married, Mr. Lotts?" Bill asked gently.

"Yes. Been married. I'm a widower now."

"I'm sorry to hear that," Bill said.

"Fifteen years ago, so there's no use being sorry, Counselor."

"Do you have children, Mr. Lotts?"

"Yes, if you want to call it that. I got three kids."

Bill glanced at Abigail, and she nodded, very slightly, as did Button. He knew what Abigail was thinking, bitter man, hates his kids, maybe never sees them—

"We accept Mr. Lotts," Bill told the judge, hoping that Lotts would remember him kindly for however many days of work the trial brought him.

"It's a risk," Ridley said afterward. "You never know what's going on in a cop's mind. They're not like us. Different world, different thinking."

"He's a cop," was Jim's only remark.

The day finished with only two jurors selected and Bill with a splitting headache. Back at the hotel, they had an hour before the press conference. Abigail had Bill stretch out on the bed. She had given him two aspirin and put a cold wet towel on his brow. Her heart went out to this big, lumbering man she had married. She had accepted the fact, long ago, that he was not as bright as she, but his love for her was so absolute that it made up for other things, for the excitement she felt had been missing from her life. Sometimes his apparent obtuseness irritated her beyond belief, and on the other hand, she was on occasion surprised by his insights. Also, he had a gift of understanding his children. They adored him.

When they first began to work out a defense, she felt, in her panic, that they should try to find the most distinguished counsel in the country. She felt that it might be wise to enlist a revered Republican conservative law firm; when Bill had gently talked her out of that, she resented his position. She had opened her heart to Button Ridley, who said to her, "No—no, my dear. Bill is right. We are not fighting points of law or simply preparing a brief for the Supreme Court—which we will do in any case—but something else that would slip away, I'm afraid, if we enlist one of those great law firms. This is the ultimate end of thousands of years of struggle by women for the right to be free, to have the final say over their own bodies."

"I know, I know. But then I am the goat tied to the tree—my God, Button, these primitives here in this state are trying to kill me."

"No."

"How can you be so sure?"

"Because you and Bill cannot go that way."

Hardly reassuring, Abigail thought, but she was right. It's you and me, old man. We'll do it together.

Bill had closed his eyes. Stretched on the bed with the wet towel on his brow, he appeared to feel better. She reminded him of the press conference.

"Yes, of course."

"How is the head?"

"Better, I think."

"Jack can't make up his mind whether or not I should talk to them or hide behind my lawyers. What do you think?"

"What does Button say?"

"She says I must talk. She says that this hiding behind counsel is bullshit."

"Right. I agree with her in this case. But be careful."

"Rest assured."

"You have done no wrong, not now, not ever—you can hold on to that." He sat up and kissed her.

4

July 6. Dede Brown, National Public Radio:

My mother, who grew up here in Clarkton, remembers a time when a black woman entered the Jackson House only through the kitchen door. Times change, even in Clarkton, although at this moment in time, the outside world may be reluctant to believe it. The Jackson House is the largest and best hotel in Clarkton, and today Stewart Cox, the manager, welcomed me with enthusiasm. Mr. Cox is a friend of the trial. He favors neither one side nor the other; he simply embraces the fact that history and Clarkton have meshed. Not only is every room in the

Jackson House rented, but practically every room has double and triple occupancy. You have to wedge your way into the bar to order a drink, and there are three dinner seatings in the dining room.

Mr. Cox has no opinions about the trial; he is a living witness to the fact that free trade lowers all barriers. I have been trying desperately for the past two weeks to get a quiet one-on-one interview with Abigail Goodman where there would be no interference and my equipment could register properly, a place where we would not be interrupted and where Professor Goodman could speak her mind. Mr. Cox finally agreed to let me use his small old-fashioned ladies' parlor, and Professor Goodman agreed to meet me there at eight o'clock in the morning. She is a guest at the hotel for the trial, while I am staying with my great-aunt Gussie near the old wagon works. Having said all this in introduction, what follows is my interview with professor Abigail Goodman.

"Professor Goodman, as a black woman here in Clarkton, I feel to some extent that I am in enemy country. Not that I am afraid of violence; but I grew up in San Francisco, and I can't help feeling that a different set of laws and rules operates here."

"No, I don't share that feeling, although I can understand completely why you have it. You see, Ms. Brown, I must make my own position clear. I have no sense of being in enemy country. I am in the United States of America, and that is a far cry from enemy country. My ancestors lived in this city since 1791, the year it was founded, and it was here that my great-grandfather put on his uniform to fight in the ranks of the Confederacy."

"Then can you explain why, Professor Goodman, they chose you to arrest and put on trial? I might state, asking this question, that I am totally of your point of view. I believe in choice, and since I am employed by National Public Radio I have no hesitation in saying so."

"The answer is very simple. My grandfather, an attorney and onetime judge in this state, fought the Klan and the rotten crew in the State House who run this state and bleed it dry and suck out its life blood. This stupid, barbaric so-called crusade against abortion is only the latest in their list of infamies."

"Professor Goodman, your subject, as I have been given to understand, is the role of women in history?"

"Yes. It is a course I devised. It's the first time such a course has been given at Hilden. The course was oversubscribed and brought on a great deal of discussion."

"And am I correct in saying that you lay special emphasis on what you call the war against women?"

"Yes."

"And is it also true that you teach that the movement against abortion is in essence a movement against the feminist revolution and that it has deep economic roots?"

"Yes, that is an essential part of my course."

"Then, Professor Goodman, could you explain your position for our listeners? I stress this point because National Public Radio has thousands of listeners in every part of the country, and

I feel that your trial goes beyond this question of whether or not abortion is the murder of a human being."

"Let me try to answer your question as simply as I can. Women are denied many rights that are given to men; these bear on questions of equality. If nature had so contrived that men as well as women could bear children, there would be no argument about choice; so the matter of choice against right to life is a question of a woman's right to make decisions concerning her body. All rights are connected, and for the subjugation of woman to continue, all rights must be denied. On our part, all rights must be fought for."

"Buy why, Professor Goodman, does this denial of rights persist?"

"The reasons are many, but let me give you one that stands out like a sore thumb. Nationally, women's wages are only sixty percent of the wages of men. In this state, women's wages are only forty-five percent of the wages of men. I would love to go on with this subject, but I'm afraid we'll be late at court. Forgive me."

I thanked Professor Goodman and concluded the interview. I had considered asking her some questions concerning the abortion she had undergone recently and which led to her indictment; but I was quite certain she would not respond to this subject and that any attempts to provoke answers might do harm to her case. National Public Radio will keep you informed each day on the progress of what some are beginning to call the most important criminal trial of our time—a trial that rivals the Scopes trial as a historical event.

They had chosen eleven jurors. Abigail kept her own list, jotting the names down on a yellow legal pad. There were four white men: Norman Lotts, the retired policeman; Huey Mantel, cashier at the local Piggly Wiggly; Fred Ashton, onetime teacher and now proprietor of the town bookshop; and Joe Biddle, a plumber's assistant. There were two black men: Morris Mc-Grath, a hospital orderly; and Oscar Butterfly, a short-order cook. There were five white women: Alice Johnson, who worked at the local Coca-Cola bottling plant; Hope Williams, housewife; Hasty Morgan, housewife; Susan Sinclair, clerk at an insurance company and only twenty-seven years old; and Georgia Kent, a stenographer.

The final juror now stood before the judge. She was a black woman, middle-aged, work-worn. Her name was Essie Lotus.

"How old are you, Mrs. Lotus?" the judge asked her.

"Forty-four years, Your Honor." She hesitated, then said, "It's Miss Essie Lotus. I never married."

"I see. Can you read and write, Miss Lotus?"

"Yes, sir. I finished high school."

"Do you work?"

"Yes, sir. I do day work. Fancy laundry, mostly."

"Would you like to serve on this jury?"

"I think I would, Your Honor."

At this point Abigail leaned over to Jack Ridley and whispered, "You know they used up their peremps."

"I'm licking my lips," Ridley said. This was the twelfth black woman Anderson had challenged.

"Mr. Anderson?" the judge said.

Charles Anderson stared at Essie Lotus without rising from behind his table. "You have any children, Essie?"

Abigail watched with interest and a small prayer as Essie Lotus's lips pressed tight.

"Would you please answer Mr. Anderson's question," Benson said.

"I am forty-four years old."

There was a long moment of silence, and then the judge said slowly, "Mr. Anderson, please address this juror as Miss Lotus."

Anderson swallowed and said, "Miss Lotus, do you have any children?"

"I have."

"How many?"

"Two. A boy and a girl."

"And, Miss Lotus, you had these children out of wedlock?"

"Yes. My man and me, we planned to marry. But he worked the river and a load hit him and kill him."

"Oh, please God," Abigail whispered. "Let her be ours."

"We challenge for cause," Anderson said.

"What cause?" the judge asked mildly.

"This is a loose woman, a woman of no character, a woman living in sin—"

"I am not!" Essie Lotus exploded.

"Enough, Miss Lotus," Benson said. "You will answer questions, that's all. Now tell me, these two children of yours, where are they?"

"My son is in New York. He is twenty-four years old. He works as a waiter during the day, and nighttime he studies at the New York University School of Pharmacology. He is going to be a druggist someday, God willing. My daughter is eighteen. She do manicure at Sadie Harris's Hairdressing, right here in town."

"Do you have any set opinions about this case?"

"No, sir. I don't have any opinions about anything until I know something about it."

"Mr. Anderson," the judge said, "I see no basis for cause." He turned to the defense. "Does the defense have basis for cause?"

"No, Your Honor," Jack Ridley said.

"You have peremptory challenges unused. Do you wish to challenge this juror?"

"No, Your Honor. We have no challenge. We accept."

The judge turned back to Anderson. "I see no reason for cause."

"This is a woman who has lived in sin."

"We are in a courtroom, Mr. Anderson, not a church. A woman is on trial for her life in this court, and I intend to conduct this trial according to the laws of this state. Miss Lotus, please take your seat in the jury box."

"I move an exception," Anderson said.

They went on to choose two alternate jurors, and then court was adjourned for the day.

Judge Benson said, "We shall begin to try this case tomorrow morning at nine o'clock. I am determined to finish this trial and put it to the jury in no more than two weeks. The prosecution will be ready with their witnesses for tomorrow."

Later, Button said to Abigail, "Please, Abby, don't get your hopes up too high on Essie Lotus. We don't know who she is or what she thinks about abortion."

July 7. Karl Benski, special to *Izvestia:*

While the whole procedure of putting a woman on trial for her life for having an abortion illustrates the uneven practice of democracy here in the United States, the adherence, even in this singular case, to the rules of trial by jury indicates a system of justice which might well be studied in Russian courts as they go about remodeling their criminal practice. I watched the selection of a jury here in Clarkton, USA, twelve men and women and two alternates, to sit in judgment on Professor Abigail Goodman. Each side, both the prosecution and the defense, is allowed to reject a certain number of potential jurors without specifying a reason. These are called peremptory challenges. They are also permitted to reject jurors for cause, as they call it, that is, for inadequacies that they perceive in the jurors. This is structured so that a jury may be found free of preconceptions of guilt or innocence.

That is not to say that in this southern town any jury can be found that is wholly free from prejudice. In my own casual questioning of men and women who live here in Clarkton, I find little sympathy for Professor Goodman. However, while people I talk to show a very warm feeling toward this Russian correspondent, now that the Cold War is over, whether they are ready to speak freely is another question.

Yet the final makeup of the jury, now chosen, is very interesting. There are black men, a black woman, housewives, workingmen, a good sampling of the community. But in a trial such as this promises to be, with its unusual complexities and its presentation of charges never before proffered in an American courtroom, one wonders about the abilities of these jurors to understand the medical and judicial problems that must be dealt with. I have not yet decided whether this system or our own system of judicial review is best suited to provide just decisions. That remains to be seen.

Abigail had never thought of herself as an orphan—not until now. She had once brought home a tape of Marion Anderson singing, "Sometimes I feel like a motherless child." Bill found her sitting and listening to it and crying. He was upset, and when he had said something to her about it and about the uselessness of it—her mother had died only months before— she had turned on him angrily. But an orphan? This was no image she had of herself until now. Now she found herself thinking, I am so damned alone, so alone; and thinking that it was no use trying to make Bill or anyone else understand what she felt.

Her father had died of cancer when she was nine years old. His body had been cremated, so Abigail had not witnessed a cemetery burial, a coffin lowered into the ground, leaving her with the knowledge that her father's body lay there. For her, he had simply disappeared. One day he bent toward her out of his bed and kissed her; the next day he was gone. No trace of him remained.

That was in the early spring of the year, and that year was the first time she had spent an entire summer in Clarkton. She had been to Clarkton with her mother and father when she was six years old, but at nine she remembered little of the earlier visit. After her father took sick, her grandparents came to New York. Now, with her father dead and her mother with a day job from nine to five, she was shipped off to Clarkton the day school finished, to remain there until school opened in the fall. She felt no resentment over this. Compared with their small New York apartment, the Henderson house, then just outside of town, surrounded by unspoiled countryside, fields and woods and down the dirt road the pond, was as close to paradise as anything Abigail had ever imagined.

She adored her grandmother, a round little woman, round-faced, round-cheeked, and just plump enough not to be fat. Her grandfather, on the other hand, was six feet four inches tall, a frosty giant of a man who found great difficulty dealing with children. It was the death of his son that broke the wall between himself and this slender child of nine years. He found that it was easier to read to her from a book than to maintain a conversation with her. The death of his son had been a terrible blow to him and to his wife, their only child, and as some men do, he swallowed his grief, encasing it in an opaque shell. He locked himself up in his study. Though he had been retired for several years, he would still take an occasional case on a pro bono basis. Now he would neither talk on the telephone nor see anyone on any legal matter.

Abigail broke through that. She knocked at the door of his study, and when she told him who was there, he opened the door and stood looking down at her. She held out a dimestore book about Peter Rabbit.

"I want you to read this book to me, please."

"Can't you read?" he demanded.

"Of course I can read. But Granny said I should ask you to read it to me."

"This book?" taking it from her.

"Yes, please."

"Well, I can't read this book. It's a silly book."

He tossed the book away and reached down and took her hand. "Come with me."

He led her upstairs to a room where the blinds were drawn. When he raised the blinds, Abigail saw a bed, neatly made, as if ready for someone to sleep that night, a bookcase across the wall facing the bed, banners on the wall, in one corner a bat, baseball glove, catcher's mask, and in another corner a pair of canoe paddles, and next to the paddles a ten-speed bike.

"You father's room," her grandfather said shortly. "Let's look at the books and find something sensible. How old are you these days?"

"I was nine just before my daddy died."

"Well, then you're not a baby. On the other hand, Leon didn't have any proper little-girl books like *Little Women* and such. But let's see what we can find."

He went down on his knees, poking along the line of books, peering at each title. "What's that?" he asked her sharply.

"*Moby Dick*," she read.

"Oh, no, no, no. Put you to sleep. Anyway, I can't read that long. *Tarzan of the Apes?*"

"I saw the movie."

"Just as well. Leon loved Tarzan. Did you know, out in California there's a town called Tarzana? Right. Named after Tarzan. Used to be part of the estate of the writer Edgar Rice Burroughs. *Tom Sawyer?*"

"Daddy read it to me."

"Did he? Now, there's *Huck Finn*—no, we'll save that. Here it is." He pulled out a book. "*Treasure Island.* Your daddy ever read that to you?"

For the next week, he read to Abigail from *Treasure Island.* Years later her grandmother told Abigail that it had saved his senses, possibly his life, too. It drew him out of the deep depression he had fallen into.

And one day Abigail said to him, "Where's my daddy?"

Henderson paused in his reading, looked at his granddaughter thoughtfully, and then closed the book and put it aside.

"You don't want to tell me?"

"Your daddy's dead, my dear. Your daddy was once my little boy. Your grandma and I had given up hope of ever having a child, and then your daddy came. I was forty-eight years old. Now I'm an old man and he's gone. Oh, not really gone. He's inside of you, and he's inside of me, and there's where he will be forever. You don't understand that now. But we'll talk about it again, and in time you'll understand about your father and how he went away."

And now, Abigail Goodman, forty-one years old herself, listened to Jack Ridley talk about her grandfather and protested that the time of her grandfather's battles was half a century ago.

"But they don't forget, Abby. This state was and is so rotten that a hundred years would make no difference. Floyd Henderson put a lieutenant governor and five state senators in jail. He made it impossible for the governor ever to run for office again, and he put away the richest and most powerful banker in the state for twenty years. That was Harlan Ludlow, and his son is our governor. So, my dear, it's all no accident. We're going to win this case, but we'll sweat blood doing it."

"And what will it cost you, Jack?"

"I don't know. Button and myself, well, we've been making a good living, eating high on the hog and fattening up. That's not good for the immortal soul."

"Rita says what business you had has run for cover."

"Rita has a big mouth."

"And you believe in an immortal soul?" Abigail asked.

"Sort of. Or maybe it's just a feeling that a man should collect a few shreds of decency along the way."

5

WHEN JUDGE BENSON took his seat for the opening of the trial and instructed the clerk to read the indictment, Bill rose with an objection.

"Mr. Goodman," the judge said, "the indictment has not yet been read."

"Yes, Your Honor. I am objecting to the reading of the indictment—"

The buzz of sound in the crowded courtroom died away.

"I am sorry. I cannot entertain such an objection, Mr. Goodman."

"May I make it for the record, Your Honor?"

The judge allowed that to hang in the air for a long moment. Then he nodded. "Yes, you may," he said softly. "I must state that I will overrule, but you may put it in the record. However, the indictment must be read. When the clerk has finished, I will hear your objection. You understand that it cannot be an objection to the reading of the indictment, since the indictment will have been read. You may object to the content of the indictment, and if that is your intent, I will hear a motion to dismiss the indictment. We do things differently here, and there are higher courts if you wish to challenge our law."

"Thank you, Your Honor," said Bill.

The judge gestured to the clerk, who rose and read: "The State against Abigail Henderson Goodman. The State hereby charges that Abigail Henderson Goodman has knowingly and willingly violated section 157 of the State's criminal code, the aforementioned section reading thus: Any adult consenting to or performing or aiding and abetting an act of abortion upon her body or the body of another woman after the first trimester of pregnancy shall be subject to criminal arrest and trial, and upon being found guilty shall be sentenced to death."

Bill stood up and said, "I object to the indictment, and I move that it be set aside and the prisoner freed for the following reasons: the first is based on the common-law understanding that an act committed upon oneself shall not be regarded as a criminal act, and we hold that the unborn embryo is an integral part of the woman accused. We do not admit that the alleged abortion was criminal either in intent or action. Second, the alleged abortion predates the governor's signing of the law under which this indictment is brought."

"We have been through that. The law of this state," the judge said, "is specified in section 157 of the criminal code. The accused is being legally tried under section 157, which bases its legality upon the concept of an embryo that has matured past the first trimester, as a person, entitled to the protection of the law."

"So be it," Abigail whispered to Button Ridley.

Bill sat down and nodded. "No damn use at all, is it."

"A clown show," Jack Ridley said. "You start with one small piece of restraint, and then it builds, like an avalanche."

The judge tapped with his gavel for silence, and Charles Anderson rose to make his opening statement. Abigail studied the jury—unmoving, open-eyed, relaxed, twelve good men and women, tried and true and ready to decide whether she should be put to death or not.

"In this case of the *State* versus *Abigail Henderson Goodman*," Anderson began, "civilization takes a long step forward. For decades now, I could say for generations, we have watched untold thousands of human lives washed out and ripped out of the wombs of women who sneer at God and at life. Little do they care about these human creatures whom they murder with abortion, casting the tiny bodies onto garbage heaps—abortion? Oh, no, ladies and gentlemen, I call it murder."

He took a deep breath, dropped his head forward, and closed his eyes—his moment of grief.

"But no more. Finally, under God's command, as Christian soldiers marching as to war, the fine, God-fearing legislators of this state have taken the step that will put an end to this murderous travesty they call abortion, once and for all. We are a state that has had capital punishment on our books and in our criminal code for many years. He who takes a life must pay for it with his own life. So saith the Lord God, and so saith the law of this sovereign state, sections 156 and 157 of the criminal code.

"And here before you, on trial for the act of murder, you see the defendant"—he turned to Abigail, lest any of the jurors should imagine that he was talking about another—"Abigail Henderson Goodman."

Anderson took out a handkerchief, wiped his brow, and posed before the jury box.

"What shall we prove with the evidence we propose to bring before you? Well, we shall prove that an abortion done after the first trimester is an act of murder. We shall prove that by the third trimester, a pregnant woman is carrying a human being in her body. And more!" he cried, raising his voice. "We shall prove that the abortion undertaken by Abigail Goodman, the defendant, was elective, that there was no medical reason for her action, but that it was an evil and vicious—"

Benson interrupted Anderson. "I would restrain myself from judgment, Mr. Anderson, and rest on the facts."

"Yes, Your Honor."

"That wretched little bastard," Jack Ridley said softly.

"We shall prove that the abortion took place, and that it was murder, premeditated and evil." He wiped his brow again and returned to the prosecution table.

Judge Benson glanced at the courtroom clock. "I think we have time for a witness. I want to move this along. Would you call your first witness, Mr. Anderson."

The first witness was Dr. Joseph Lang. The notes on Abigail's pad described him as chief of obstetrics at Heart of Mercy Hospital at the state capital. He was a small, neat man, dressed in a white suit, white buck shoes, with a few dozen long strands of hair combed over a bald skull. He appeared uneasy and unsure of himself, but less so when the testimony began.

As he seated himself, Anderson handed a sheaf of papers to the judge and asked that they be entered as evidence.

"The records from Hilden Hospital," Bill told Abigail.

The clerk offered the Bible to the witness, and he took the oath.

"Would you state your name and title," Anderson said.

"Dr. Joseph Lang. I am chief of obstetrics at Heart of Mercy Hospital."

"And how long have you held that post?"

"Seven years. But I have been at the hospital twenty-two years."

"Then I might say you are thoroughly versed in your profession."

"I think you could."

The judge had passed the papers to the clerk, and now Anderson took them and handed them to Dr. Lang, asking him to glance through them.

"Would you tell the jury what you have there?"

"Yes. Certainly. These are faxed copies of—here, this is the admission record of Abigail Goodman's admission to Hilden Hospital for elective surgery. This sheet is a medical description of the surgery performed by Dr. Percy Simpson on the tenth of May—by his calculation on the ninety-first day after conception. Apart from election by the person involved, Mrs. Goodman, no medical reasons are given for the abortion. The abortion, again according to these records, was carried out successfully with no complications."

"Except the death of the child?"

Jack Ridley rose to object.

"Just watch it," the judge said to Anderson. "The objection is sustained."

"Yes, the death of the embryo," the doctor said.

"Would you object—scientifically, of course—to my calling the embryo a child?"

"No, I would not."

"Because ninety-one days is well after the end of the first trimester?"

"Exactly." Then he added, "By my reckoning."

"I think your reckoning is satisfactory and professional. Could you, Dr. Lang, tell us—that is, the jury—something about this process of birth? Not that we don't all know how birth occurs, but you could refresh us, could you not?"

"Certainly. We begin with fertilization. I don't think I have to be very explicit about this. With this, the menstrual cycle is suppressed. Normally, the uterine lining would be shed, but the embryo prevents this. After the passage of some forty-three or forty-four days, a tiny, newly formed embryo has appeared within the amniotic sac, which protects it. The little child is now living inside the mother's body, and if you put the mother through X ray, you would see the little head, the brain, the chest, the spine, legs, hands—"

"Do you see what he's doing?" Abigail whispered to Button.

"Only too well."

"—and by ten weeks, this little child is there, right there in the womb."

"A human child?"

"Just as human as you and me, Mr. Anderson. Just as human."

"And if you were to abort this child in the eighty-fourth day of the pregnancy, what would you call that, Dr. Lang?"

"I would call it murder," the doctor said.

And Anderson, turning to the defense table, said, "Your witness, Mr. Ridley."

Jack Ridley unrolled a sheet of paper, thirty by thirty-six inches, handed it to the judge, and asked that it be entered as evidence and then passed around the jury box, so that the jurors might acquaint themselves with it. "What you will see," Ridley said, "is a pregnancy visual issued by the National Health Service in Washington."

When the jurors had finished examining the visual, Ridley passed it on to Lang.

"Would you look at it, please, sir?" Ridley said.

"I am quite familiar with this poster."

"Would you call it medically correct?"

"As far as it goes, yes."

"And looking at the chart and at the picture—that is, at the open-womb sketch of the embryo at thirteen weeks—would you take note of the embryo?"

Then Ridley took the poster and asked the judge whether he might display it to the jury again. Then he said to Lang, "Thirteen weeks is within the first trimester—that is, thirteen weeks adds up to ninety-one days. Is that not so?"

"Not by my reckoning, no sir."

"Well, let's look at this chart again. According to the numbers on this chart, the pregnancy comes to maturity and birth in thirty-eight weeks, give or take a few days, since no pregnancy is of the same duration. But note that this government visual states that usually the embryo is ready for birth at the end of thirty-eight weeks or thirty-nine weeks. If we divide thirty-eight weeks by three, we get ninety-one days. If we add the extra week, the first trimester extends to ninety-two and one-third days. Will you agree?"

"No, sir. I will not. The first trimester is ninety-one days, no more, no less."

"When Mr. Anderson said that ninety-one days was well after the first trimester, you agreed with him. But even by your own reckoning, Mr. Anderson's statement is untrue, as is your support of it."

"No, sir."

Ridley walked back to the defense table, picked up a pile of five large books, and took them to the judge's desk. "These are five of the leading books on obstetrics. The volume on top is

Williams' Obstetrics. Dr. Williams, at Johns Hopkins University, where he taught some years ago, was considered the leading authority in America on the subject. We have inserted markers and underlined the passages I intend to refer to."

Anderson leaped up with an objection. "Your Honor, he is introducing witnesses who cannot be cross-examined."

"No, Your Honor. Even Mr. Anderson must realize that I can quote statements without cross-examination. His objection is ridiculous, and it turns this court into a joke."

"Save your comments about the court, Mr. Ridley," Benson said, a note of anger in his voice.

"Can I quote the Bible without God in the witness box?" Ridley demanded.

"That's enough!" Benson snapped. "Get on with your cross-examination."

"Dr. Lang," Ridley said, handing one of the books to the witness, "Would you open to the page indicated."

Again Anderson objected.

"You're overruled," the judge said. "Let him make his point without any more objections."

"Would you read the underlined passage."

Lang looked at the judge.

"Read it."

Lang read: "To pinpoint the exact hour or day of conception is to all effects impossible."

Abigail watched with interest as Ridley walked over to the jurors' box, let his glance move across the faces of the jurors, turned then to face Lang, and asked quietly, "Do you agree with Dr. Williams's statement, Dr. Lang?"

So it went, and so it would go, and Abigail Goodman thought of all the times she had watched the same movements in a hundred films and plays. She had studied the faces of the jurors long enough to expect nothing, even from Essie Lotus. How many Essies had she known here in Clarkton? How many would put their heads in the lion's mouth?

"Will you answer the question, Dr. Lang? Do you agree or not?"

"Well, I'm not sure that there's any simple answer."

"It's a very simple question. Do you agree?"

"No, I do not," Lang answered resolutely. "I have treated too many women who were able to tell me the exact moment of their conception."

"Since all of these eminent authorities on obstetrics agree that the moment of conception cannot be known, you are willing to set yourself up against them? Is that so?"

"Yes."

"A man of courage." Jack Ridley picked up his notes. "A moment ago, you told Mr. Anderson something about forty-three days after conception." He turned to the stenographer. "Could you read that passage?"

The stenographer read, "After the passage of some forty-three or forty-four days, a tiny, newly formed embryo has appeared within the amniotic sac, which protects it. The little child is now living inside the mother's body, and if you put the mother through X ray, you would see the little head, the brain, the chest, the spine, legs, hands, and by ten weeks, this little child is there, right there in the womb."

"That's enough," Ridley said. "Now, Dr. Lang, isn't this a complete fabrication?"

"No, it is not."

"Isn't this a pseudoscientific absurdity?"

"No, sir."

"Does the embryo at forty-four days have arms, legs? Does it? I hold up this visual distributed by the United States government. Will you look at the detailed drawing of an embryo at forty-three days? Do you see arms, legs, eyes—how big is that embryo at forty-three days?"

Dr. Lang stared ahead of him without answering.

"How big? This big?" Ridley held up his hand, thumb and forefinger about an inch and a half apart.

"You are to answer that question, Dr. Lang," the judge said.

"Yes."

"Yes what? One inch? Two inches?"

"Perhaps."

"Perhaps one inch, perhaps two inches." Ridley handed the poster to Lang. "There's the diagram. Show me the arms and the legs, Dr. Lang."

Lang turned away from the diagram without speaking.

"Well, speak up, Dr. Lang! Where are the eyes, the mouth, the brain?" Ridley took the poster and gave it to Norman Lotts, the ex-policeman, who was foreman of the jury. Then he turned to Dr. Lang and said angrily, "I put it to you, sir, that every word you have spoken here is a lie! Is that not so?"

"No! I gave good, truthful evidence."

"I put it to you that the only purpose of your testimony is to indict my client, and that you were paid for this. Is that not so?"

"No, not at all."

"I am asking you how much you were paid for this testimony."

Anderson was halfway to the bench with his objection. "He does not have to answer that!"

"I see you make the law now, Mr. Anderson," the judge said. "Witnesses are paid. That has been going on for a long time, here as well as elsewhere. Answer the question, Dr. Lang."

Lang swallowed, bit his lip, and said, "Two thousand dollars."

"And who paid you this very substantial fee?" Ridley asked.

"National Anti-abortion."

"And when was this money paid to you, Dr. Lang?"

"Do I have to answer that?" Lang asked the judge plaintively.

Anderson was on his feet. "When the money was paid to him has no bearing whatsoever on this case."

"How can that be, Mr. Anderson?" the judge asked.

"Because this is cross-examination. I never introduced the question of payment."

"Mr. Anderson, you're floundering," Benson said with impatience. "You introduced the witness. He is your witness. Mr. Ridley has every right to know how much he was paid and by whom—and when."

"I take exception."

"Noted." Benson turned to Lang. "Answer the question, Dr. Lang."

"May twelfth."

There was a rustle of voices throughout the courtroom, and half a dozen newspapermen and -women pushed their way out of the media rows and ran for the exits. The judge pounded his desk and demanded order.

"The low bastards," Button hissed. "They tapped our phones."

"What are you talking about?" Abigail wanted to know. "This is insane—May twelfth."

"The day after you telephoned us," Button said, "and told us you might drive down."

Now Benson pointed to Anderson. "Both of you—you, Mr. Anderson and you, Mr. Ridley—approach the bench."

The two lawyers walked up to the judge's rostrum.

"Do you know what I'm going to do?" Benson whispered. "I am going to allow this witness to complete his testimony. I want the jury to hear what he has to say, and I want to hear what he has to say. Now as for you, Ridley, I know damn well what's on your mind. You intend to call for a mistrial. And you, Anderson, you're going to start screaming for exceptions. I would suggest that at this moment both tactics are wrong. When we finish with this witness, we'll break for lunch. Then I'll see both of you in my chambers at two o'clock."

"You're asking me to leave hanging the fact that a man is paid to be a witness in a trial not yet in existence, of a woman not yet indicted, who is not in this town—is that what you're asking me, Your Honor?"

"Ridley, for Christ's sake, I'm only asking you to go back and finish your cross-examination."

"As an officer of the court—" Ridley began.

Benson stopped him short. "Just hold it right there, and don't give me that crap about being an officer of the court. I brought both of you up here because I did not want a fight out front on mistrials and exceptions. I think we all want to hear what this witness has to say in the way of an explanation, and I am determined to proceed."

Meanwhile, at the defense table, Button Ridley was spelling it out for Abigail, Bill, and Jim Cooper. "It's no great mystery," Button said. "They must have had a tap on our office phone for God only knows how long. Why? Because we're the kind of law firm we are, and because we take more civil rights cases than any firm in the state. When Abigail called and said she was going to try to talk you into an auto trip down here and that she had just come through an abortion, and when you spoke to Jack"—turning to Bill—"and told him that Abigail had been through this ordeal at Hilden Hospital, but was all right now, well, there's someone up in the Hilden branch of National Anti-abortion who keeps track of people and names. That's all they had to know. The whole thing was put into motion, entrapment and all that goes with it."

The judge and the lawyers returned to the courtroom. The constable ordered the spectators and jury to stand and then to sit. Benson, grim-faced, tapped with his gavel. When he achieved silence in the overexcited audience, he reminded Dr. Lang that he was still under oath.

"Dr. Lang," Jack Ridley said, "I asked you before whether you were paid to be a witness in this trial, and you replied that you were. I then asked you what you had been paid as a witness, and you answered that you have been paid two thousand dollars. Is that true?"

"Yes, sir," Dr. Lang mumbled.

"Talk up!" the judge told him.

"Yes, sir," louder.

"And then I asked you when this payment had taken place, and you replied that it was May twelfth. I presume of this year. Is that not correct?"

"Yes."

"Very well. Since the twelfth of May predates the indictment of Abigail Goodman, who is on trial here, and since the twelfth of May predates the arrival of Mr. and Mrs. Goodman here in this town, I will ask you to explain how you came to be a witness in this case?"

Abigail was puzzled by the fact that Lang was not as disconcerted as he might have been, considering the situation. Indeed, his reply was glib and well rehearsed.

"I have a reputation in the state," he said, "of being one of the leading medical advocates of the Right to Life cause. When the law under which Mrs. Goodman is being tried was passed by the state legislature, the state Anti-abortion League retained me to be an expert witness the first time the law was put into active use. That is why I am here. Regardless of who had been indicted, I would have been called as a witness for the prosecution."

July 17. Freda Hammond, special to *The Times* of London:

Today we heard the first witness to be called in this extraordinary trial, one Joseph Lang, a physician who practices in the capital of the state. His testimony, to the effect of a ninety-one-day-old embryo being a full-fledged undersize person, was torn to shreds by Jack Ridley, one of the defense attorneys. But for a British observer, the interesting element today was the behavior of the judge, George Lee Benson. He holds himself impartially aloof, yet it appears evident, at least to this observer, that he is totally disgusted at being placed in the position he occupies. This is only my impression, but inquiring into the judge's background, I was told that during the 1960s, when the great civil rights struggles took place in the southern states of America, as a young lawyer, he acted for the defense in a number of cases where black people were brought to trial for breaking the apartheid regulations of the time.

This led me to inquire how it was that the chief justice of the state had assigned him to sit on this case, and the answers I received indicated that the indictment was so outrageous that the governor felt it necessary to balance the scales of justice with a judge who posessed a reputation for integrity.

I also learned that the governor and the leadership in the state legislature did not consider any real possibility of a jury verdict for Professor Goodman, the defendant. The governor ran for office on a platform that promised extreme punishment for illegal abortion, on top of an existing statute that outlawed all abortion in the state; and since he was voted into office by a sizable majority, he appears to be quite confident that the people will support a guilty verdict in the case of Abigail Goodman.

The possible effect of this nationally is enormous. I am told that fourteen states of the Union have ready severe anti-abortion laws, waiting to be presented to the state legislatures for passage; and some of the American reporters, familiar with this long struggle, tell me that in at least six of the states passage of these anti-abortion bills is practically certain. There is not yet any indication that penalties will be as severe as here in this state, but that of course remains to be seen.

6

THE DEFENSE attorneys had been given a small room, off to one side of the courtroom, where they could lunch without fighting their way through the cameras and the reporters. Jim Cooper had ordered sandwiches, and he found an electric coffee maker. But when Bill and Abigail and the Ridleys entered the room, Millicent Woolton and Eileen Mott of the *New York Globe* were already waiting for them.

"Press conference," Millicent said. "It's a must."

"No, we don't have the time," Bill said.

"It's bursting wide open. Don't you see that?" Millicent argued.

"I will say this, if you'll listen to me for a moment." Eileen Mott was desperately sincere. "I've been on this job twelve years, and this is the biggest story that has ever come my way. You're in a cocoon down here. You can't possibly imagine what an international incident this has become. You can't hide from the press, and you can't rest on one interview with National Public Radio."

Jack Ridley shook his head. "We don't have time."

Abigail said, "She's right, you know. We'll try to make time—somehow."

Jim Cooper came into the room, carrying a quart container of ice cream and half a dozen plastic plates. "You white folks sitting here and stuffing yourself, and I'm out there sweating in the hot sun." He saw Millicent and the *Globe* writer at that moment and dropped his accent. Then he took Jack aside and said, "Please, Mr. Ridley, get rid of them. We have to talk."

"I heard that," Millicent said. "That's the wrong road. Don't get rid of us. Talk to us."

"Tonight," Bill said. "I promise you. Millicent, we'll have a press conference tonight, but keep it down to twenty people."

"Where?"

"Your office, Jack? Eight o'clock?"

"Sure."

Abigail ushered them out, pleading for their patience.

Eileen Mott said, "You're sitting on the hottest seat in the country."

When they had gone, Button said, "Why do I feel that we're on a train going a hundred miles an hour around a curve with no one driving?"

"Because that's where we are," Abigail agreed.

"Come on, come on," Jack Ridley said. "Let's get down to business."

Button was spooning out ice cream.

"Tell us," Jack said.

"No Sweet Sue." The words were blurred by a mouth full of ice cream. "That's the bad news."

"What!"

"No Sweet Sue. She lit out for places and parts unknown after Omi told her she was to be a witness."

"Why the hell did he have to tell her? We could have subpoenaed her at the last minute."

"No, you couldn't, and you know that," Button said. "Don't jump all over Jim. We can still use her name in the cross-examination."

Calmly eating his ice cream, Jim said, "I got more."

"Don't diddle us!" Jack said angrily.

"I just want to finish my ice cream." He grinned at Abigail. "Three years of law school, Ms. Goodman, I did my level best to be a proper white boy with a dark skin. It's hard. But believe me, I do wish to God Sweet Sue had not run for cover, not that I blame her. She wants to live. We all want to live." He put aside the ice cream. "Ladies and gentlemen, twenty-six years ago Dr. Joseph Lang did abortions."

"What!"

"Come on!"

"Jim, what in hell are you saying?" Jack wanted to know.

"What I'm saying is what I'm saying."

"All right," Bill said. "For God's sake, tell us what you have."

"I'm delighted to. This, I am told, was twenty-six years ago, downstate at the capital. There was a black Baptist preacher, name of J. Martin Luther Jones, hard as a rock, honest as the day is long—so they tell me—but narrow. No charity, no give. Right was right and wrong was wrong, and there was nothing in between."

Jack nodded. "I remember him. He was put in jail in the big civil rights struggles of the sixties. A very tough customer. His name was Jasper. He took the Martin Luther after Dr. King was murdered."

"That's right," Jim said. "And he has a daughter who was the apple of his eye, or maybe the dove out of the *Song of Songs*— they tell me pretty as a picture—and being flesh and blood, she got herself caught."

"You mean pregnant?"

"That's what they call it, and with a worthless bum, so there was no question of marriage, and the only one who knew about it was her momma, who discovered her trying to do her-self in with a bottle of aspirin, because she'd rather be dead than face her father. Her momma agreed with her, and I guess her momma would rather be dead than face Martin Luther Jones. So her momma went to this feller, whom she knew from some other incident, and pleaded with him to help her. He did that, and because Momma didn't have a nickel of her own, this feller took three thousand dollars in cash money and paid for a real doctor, so that the abortion could be done properly, and the silly child lived through it and all was well, and she went on and grew up to be a happily married and proper lady."

There was a long silence after Jim Cooper finished speaking, and finally Jack said softly, "Well, I'll be damned."

Abigail said, "God help me, I can't do it!"

"What?" Bill demanded.

"Make a point by destroying this woman."

"All right, Abby. You don't think this feller gave Dr. Lang her real name?"

"He wouldn't, would he?"

"No way. Jane Smith. Jane Doe."

"But that makes her worthless as a witness," Bill said.

"We don't want her as a witness. It's the savior who'll be our witness."

"You know who he is?"

"Of course I know who he is. Where do you think I got this story?" Jim demanded.

"Where did you get it? And who's the witness?"

"Baron Omi," Jim said smugly.

"Oh, come on!" Jack exploded. "You're not giving us that pimp again! You want us to believe that he put out three thousand dollars to save the preacher's daughter? Come on, Jim. You're writing fairy tales."

"No, I'm not writing fairy tales, but goddamn it, you live cheek and jowl with us all your lives, and you don't know one damn thing about us. Black is black and white is white. Well, it ain't! Why did Omi do it? Maybe to save his own soul, but you never set foot into a colored church, so you wouldn't know what

I mean. Maybe because he admired the preacher. Maybe because the whole civil rights struggle could mean something even to a pimp. Maybe for ten other reasons. How do I know? But he told me this, and I believe him."

"It's no good if he won't testify," Bill said.

"If he testifies," Button said, speaking for the first time, "it shatters Lang's testimony. Will he testify?"

"That's what he said." Jim nodded. "I believe him."

"Then we save that for our own case. What do you want to do with Lang when we go back into court? He's still under cross."

"If Omi testifies," Bill said, "we have to give his name to Anderson. But I wouldn't bring in his name this afternoon; you can make some points by beating around it."

"I was thinking the same thing," Jack said.

"Okay. Let's go with it."

"Still, remember," Button said, "that maybe we want him to testify and maybe we don't. I'm not impugning anything, Jim, and you've done wonders, but if we put a pimp on the stand, Anderson will tear him to shreds."

"Omi?" Jim shrugged. "That'll be something. Mr. Anderson tearing Omi to shreds. I would just like to see that! Omi knows where every skeleton in this town is hidden, and don't think a horny little devil like Anderson—forgive me the expression—hasn't indulged in his trade."

"We'll see," Jack Ridley said.

At two o'clock, Ridley and Anderson faced Judge Benson in his chambers. The judge sat at his desk in silence for a minute or so, staring at the two men; then he pointed a finger at Charles

Anderson and said, "Charley, I never thought about you as any great legal brain, but I was under the impression that you were trying to make this clown show sound valid. God knows I am. Now how in hell did you come up with Lang?"

"We thought he'd make a good witness."

"By hiring him before there was even an indictment?"

"We didn't think it would come out."

"God help us." The judge sighed and turned to Ridley. "You are going to go out there and ask for a mistrial, Jack, and you might as well know that I am not going to grant a mistrial. At this point, the whole world is watching us, and do you know what I feel like?"

"No, sir."

"I feel like I'm pissing in front of the White House, with every camera on earth watching. That's how I feel, and I am not happy. So I tell you this—the trial will go on, and both of you get out there and act like lawyers, and get this damn thing over with."

Back at the defense table, Jack shook his head to the whispered questions. "Nothing," he hissed. "We're drowning, and that cold bastard didn't even throw us a stick of wood to hang on to."

But when the time came for Dr. Lang to take the witness stand again, Ridley ran his fingers through his red hair, nodded at the jury as if to say, "There he is. Let's listen and enjoy it," and then approached Dr. Lang, his face inches from the witness's face. Before he spoke, Anderson objected.

"Intimidating the witness."

"Let the witness breathe, Mr. Ridley," the judge said.

Through the days here in Clarkton, Abigail had become increasingly fond of Jack Ridley, reversing her initial opinion of him as a horny male animal that would come on to any attractive woman. In some ways he reminded her of her grandfather; in other ways he was quite different, certainly in appearance, his heavy intimidating stance, combined with a courtroom manner of solid hesitation before he spoke—not uncertainty, but more of a warning, a hint of anger that was slow, ominous, and always low key, and then a rich low voice, very southern.

For herself, she was the silent observer, a woman on trial for her life in a contest that appeared to have no relation to her as herself, Abigail Goodman. Or to abortion, either. Here, as never before, she saw the confirmation of her belief that abortion was not the issue, that no one gave a tinker's dam about the fetus, that it was purely a contest for power, a battle fought on the fringes. The central struggle was elsewhere, at the state capital and indeed in the capital of the United States—a battle reaching for support into the darkest superstitions and subjugations of the past, fighting for control of half of the human race, clawing for control of the bodies of women, who had made their first feeble gestures toward freedom, and using that control as a step toward controlling everything else.

So she watched and bore witness with her own body as Jack Ridley said to the judge, "No, Your Honor, I am not through with this"—the pause he used so effectively, intimating that he would name the creature on the stand a witness only as a courtesy—"this witness."

"Then please continue."

Abigail glanced at Bill. After the first few days, she had come to worry more about Bill than about herself. Bill had always cast himself as her defender, her faithful and true servant, a rock to lean on—but here was Jack Ridley fighting the battle. It wasn't only that Bill lacked competence as a litigator; he was a stranger in this land, and it was certainty and color that he lacked. He was a quiet man.

Ridley's attitude toward Lang spelled out like this: "You, Lang, are poor white trash. I despise you, but I stoop to use you." Bill would not understand that, but he recognized this and never challenged Jack's position as the litigator. When Abigail asked him, "Don't you want a part of it?" he replied that Jack was better: "All I want is to get you out of this hellish place."

For Abigail, it was not simply a hellish place. It was her beginnings and memories, hellish and terrible and heartbreaking as well.

Ridley had walked away from the witness, over to the jury box; leaning against it, he said matter-of-factly, "Have you ever performed abortions, Dr. Lang?"

It took Lang a moment. "Good heavens, no!"

"No?" asked Ridley. "Didn't you tell me that you had been chief of obstetrics at Heart of Mercy Hospital?"

"I did."

"And in all those years, you were never called upon to abort a fetus through a surgical section or otherwise—even to save a patient's life? Is that what you are telling me, sir?"

"No. Of course not."

"Then you have engaged in such abortions?"

"They are not abortions."

"No? Then what are they, Dr. Lang?"

"Emergency invasive procedures."

"Come on, doctor! You hide your head in a few medical words."

"I have answered your question."

"So you have," Jack agreed. He turned to study the jury for a long moment, then swung back and snapped at Lang, "Have you ever performed abortions as abortions to prevent the birth of a child?"

Anderson rose with an objection. "What is this, Your Honor? Dr. Lang is not on trial."

"Are you fishing?" the judge demanded of Ridley.

"No, Your Honor."

"I hope you are not," the judge said thinly. "Go ahead, but watch your step."

"Would you instruct him to answer my question, Your Honor? I asked him whether he had ever performed an abortion as an abortion to prevent the birth of a child."

"Answer the question."

"I object," Anderson pleaded. "He is not on trial."

"I am not putting him on trial," Jack said. "He sits there as a professional witness. I am challenging his integrity."

"With what cause?" the judge demanded. "What do you have?"

"A witness I intend to call for the defense."

"Suppose we talk in my chambers," Benson said. And then he tapped with his gavel and adjourned the court until three o'clock. In his chambers Benson said, "Now what are you getting at, Ridley?"

"I'm going to impugn this witness because I have reasonable cause to believe that twenty-six years ago, he performed at least one illegal abortion."

"That's ridiculous," Anderson said. "The man has a record as pure as the driven snow."

"Oh, come off it," the judge said. "No one has a record as pure as the driven snow. If you thought, Anderson, that you could work your way through this as you would in a normal trial, you're very mistaken. I want to keep this legal, if such a thing is humanly possible. Now, Ridley, you say you have a witness to your charge. What kind of witness? A woman?"

"I intend to call the man who paid off Dr. Lang."

"And you have this man?" the judge asked.

"Yes."

"But to what end? Lang is not on trial."

"Lang is witness for the purpose of defining an abortion as an act of willful murder. What is his testimony worth, if I can prove him an abortionist?"

"I want the name of your witness," Anderson snapped.

"Can it wait until I present for the defense?"

"Like hell it can!" Anderson snapped.

"I'm afraid he's right, Jack," the judge said. "You opened the can of beans. I'm going to instruct you to name your witness."

"All right," Ridley agreed. "His name is Baron Omi."

Anderson began to laugh. "The pimp? You're kidding."

"Like hell I am."

"Now listen to me," the judge said. "You want to call this Baron Omi as a witness, you do so. As far as Dr. Lang is concerned, no more pushing around in the dark. If you have legitimate cross, use it. Otherwise, we go on."

Back in the courtroom, Jack said, "I have no other questions for this witness."

The prosecutor was calling his second witness, who seated himself in the witness box and took the oath.

"Will you state your name, sir," Anderson said.

"Jason Lee Homer, doctor of divinity."

"You are also a Baptist preacher, are you not?"

"I am, but that does not mean that I subscribe to or belong to any association of Baptist ministries. I honor them and give them their due, but my church is the wide and fruitful plains, the fruitful fields, the snow-clad mountains of this holy land, which the Lord God gave to the people of the United States. No roof lies upon my ministry, no walls contain my words."

"What you mean is that you are a television pastor?" Anderson asked.

"Television? What a poor word, sir! My voice goes out to those who would believe, who would be saved, and the good God permits them to look upon my face as they hear my words. Call it television if you will. I call it God's grace."

"Reverend," the judge said, "when a question is put to you

which calls for a yes or no answer, the court would appreciate such an answer. You are in a witness chair, not in the pulpit."

"My church is where I am," Pastor Homer said.

"And how large is your audience, Pastor?" Anderson asked.

"We function with five transmitters in twelve states. My churchgoers number into the tens of millions."

"And how do you know the size of your audience?"

"I subscribe to the Nielsen rating system."

Anderson let that sink in, facing the jury with modest acknowledgment of numbers so great. "And, sir," he went on to say, "what is your opinion of abortion?"

"Abortion is murder."

"Are there no exceptions to that conclusion?"

"Abortion is the murder of innocents."

"And if the mother has AIDS?"

"The child born with AIDS is an innocent."

"So you admit to no exceptions to your designation of abortion as murder?" Anderson asked.

"None."

"And what do you feel is the source of your feelings about abortion?"

"The will of God. I am his humble servant. I walk barefoot in the steps of my Master, and my heart hears the words of His Son. I stand naked, asking only that God show me the way, and my prayers are answered."

At this point Bill said to Jack, "Why don't we object? What he believes is of no moment. He could believe that the earth is flat. This is all irrelevant."

Ridley rose. Anderson paused in his questioning of the witness, stood silent for a long moment—until the judge said, "What is it, Mr. Ridley?"

"Your Honor, we are dealing with a law, perhaps with the legal validity of the law; but essentially we are dealing with a law and with the question of whether that law was broken, namely numbers 156 and 157 of the criminal code. In other words, we are dealing with evidence."

"Is that the essence of your objection, Mr. Ridley—considering of course that you intend to make an objection? Is it your purpose to make an objection?"

"Yes, sir."

"Then make it," the judge said, "and please refrain from instructing me on the rules of evidence."

"Yes, Your Honor," Jack said slowly, and Abigail realized that he was desperate in terms of a connection between himself and the judge, a kind of desperation that she sensed without understanding. Button met her eyes, nodded very slightly. Perhaps Button knew what she herself did not know. Bill stood up to whisper to Ridley.

"Are you both making this objection?" Benson asked caustically. "If not, would one of you sit down."

"Please, Bill," Jack whispered, "I know him—please let me play it."

Bill sat down. Abigail had a feeling that he was raging inside himself. One hand was shaking; he held it with the other. Abigail tried to catch his eye, but he avoided looking at her.

Jack Ridley said carefully, "I object, Your Honor, to this testimony and to any testimony that defines the indictment of my client as a sin. It is irrelevant and has no place in this trial. We are not a religious court or some ecclesiastical star chamber."

"Mr. Ridley," the judge said, "the indictment specifies abortion, does it not?"

"Yes, Your Honor, it does—but not sin."

"Mr. Ridley," Benson said slowly, "I am going to overrule your objection and suggest that you take exception. I am also going to brood on your point. Rest assured that when I instruct the jury, I shall be very precise on the question of crime versus sin. Meanwhile, I intend to allow clerical witness to have their say."

"This is insane," Bill whispered to Button.

"No—no. There's something here."

"What? Tell me what! Why the hell doesn't Jack demand a mistrial?"

"Bill, Bill," Abigail begged him, "please—don't make yourself sick over this. We're only just beginning."

"Does your television pastorate agree with you on the subject of abortion?" Anderson asked, picking up the questioning.

"They do."

"And upon what do you base your assertion that your audience agrees with you?"

"On the hundreds of thousands of letters that pour in, all of them blessing my anti-abortion work and declaring that an abortion is murder and a sin against God."

Anderson held up a sheaf of mail. "I have twelve letters here, one from each of the states where the Reverend Homer preaches. I would like to enter them as evidence. State's exhibit, number one." He passed the letters up to the judge, who glanced at them briefly and then gave them back to Anderson, who handed them to the clerk. When they had been entered, Anderson handed the letters to Homer.

"These were letters addressed to you and received by you via the United States Post Office?"

"Yes—absolutely."

"All of them received on the same day?"

"Yes, the same day."

"How many letters were received on that day?"

"Seven hundred and eleven."

"How were these twelve letters chosen?"

"At random by postmark, one from each state where our signal is clearly viewed."

"Would you select one of the letters and read it."

Jack Ridley rose to object. "This is the most blatant hearsay. These letters are not validated. We don't know who wrote them. There is no way of cross-examination."

"You can examine them," Anderson said. "We have no objection to that."

"The witness is under oath," Benson said, his voice as cold as ice.

Anderson took the letters from Homer and handed them to Jack. The letters were passed across the defense table and read.

"They constitute nothing," Ridley told the judge, "not proof of anything, not evidence."

"Give me the letters," the judge said.

Abigail read in the letter handed to her: "Dear Reverend Homer, God bless you in your crusade against this work of the devil, this slaying of innocents—"

Benson signaled for the lawyers to approach the bench. "Mr. Anderson," he said to the prosecutor, "it appears to me that you have not read the indictment. I gave you leeway with Dr. Lang, but this witness is totally beside the point. We are not here in this court with abortion on trial. Abigail Henderson Goodman is on trial. The legislator of this state has already decided that abortion after the first trimester of pregnancy is an act of murder. The fact in question is whether or not Mrs. Goodman underwent an abortion before or after her first trimester in the pregnancy. The whole world is watching this performance. We can at least try to conduct a civilized trial and a rational one."

Anderson did not budge, demanding to know what he was to do with his witness.

"I shall instruct the jury to disregard the entire testimony of the Reverend Jason Lee Homer. If you wish to question him concerning the point in question, the trimester—"

"No, Your Honor," Anderson whispered, speaking through teeth clenched in anger.

The judge then said to the jurors, "You will disregard the testimony of the witness up to this point." And to the prosecutor, "If you have additional questions for the witness, please proceed."

"Yes, Your Honor." Anderson stood still a moment or two, and then he said to Homer, "Reverend, are you familiar with the new law of this state on the subject of abortion?"

"I think I am, sir. I have battled for the right to life—"

"A simple yes or no will be sufficient," Benson said sourly.

"Yes."

"And you understand that the law states that an abortion undertaken electively after the first trimester of the pregnancy has been concluded is punishable by death."

"I do."

"And do you agree with the justice of this law?"

"I do. Such is the word of God. An eye for an eye, a tooth for a tooth."

"Your witness," Anderson said to Ridley.

Jack rose and stared at Homer thoughtfully. Then he said, "Reverend Homer, what is your net worth?"

Anderson was on his feet. "There is no connection with the direct."

"It goes to his statement that he stands barefoot and walks naked."

"All of which you disallowed," Anderson told the judge.

"Nevertheless," Benson said, "it goes to the character of the witness as a clergyman."

"What on earth has wealth to do with the character of a clergyman?" Anderson demanded.

"I am not inclined toward theological arguments. I'll allow the question. Please answer the question, Reverend Homer."

"Well, I really do not know what my net worth is. I prefer to walk unencumbered by the trappings of wealth. I hardly inquire into what few dollars I provide for myself."

"Reverend, is it true that your wife holds stocks and bonds to the value of nine million dollars?"

"Some amount like that, yes."

"And is it true that she holds a sixty percent interest in the resort known as Our Heavenly Rest?"

"Yes, I think so."

"And is it true that you drive a Mercedes and that your wife drives a Rolls-Royce?"

"Yes."

"And isn't it also true that the money for all this wealth owned by your wife came from devoted listeners to your television program?"

"A gift to me is a token of God's love."

"Yes. And you set yourself up to judge a woman dying of AIDS who aborts an embryo?"

"Sin is not measured by wealth."

"Reverend Homer, who is Sweet Sue? Did you pay for her abortion?" Ridley demanded in what was almost a snarl.

Homer appeared to collapse into himself. Anderson leaped to his feet with an objection, and the judge said to the jury, "You will ignore Mr. Ridley's last question."

"I have no other questions for this witness," Jack said.

Benson motioned for them to approach the bench, and when they stood before him, he said to Ridley, "What in hell do you think you're doing in this court, Mr. Ridley? This is not a circus. Now who the hell is Sweet Sue?"

"Can we talk in chambers?"

Judge Benson adjourned the court until the following day. Jack said to Abigail, "Trust me, Abby. I'm beginning to see a flicker of light at the end of this lousy tunnel." And turning to Bill, "If it's all right with you, I think I should go into chambers alone."

Bill hesitated.

"No, Bill must go with you," Abigail said, thinking that it was as much her marriage here on trial as her life, thinking that the balance between these two men was close to getting out of hand.

Button sensed the same thing. "Jack, no," she said. "You're going to talk about Sweet Sue. Bill must be there. It's not proof of anything, but it makes a shared fact."

Bill gripped Jack's arm. "Jack, you're running this trial. I don't want to screw it up. If it's better alone—"

"No," Abigail interrupted. "This is a joint thing. For God's sake don't keep him waiting."

Anderson was already in chambers when Jack and Bill appeared. The judge was writing. Now he pointed his pen at Ridley and said, "Explain, and it had better be a damn good explanation."

"We located a young woman, a black woman, who for a while had been Reverend Homer's mistress. He made her pregnant and paid for her abortion—sent her north to a clinic in Ohio where the abortion was performed."

"If that's so," the judge said, "and nothing surprises me anymore—but if that's so and you intend to call this young

105

woman as a witness, why didn't you give her name to Mr. Anderson?"

"We intended to, but she has gone to ground and we can't locate her."

"I see. So for want of a witness, you threw her name at the Reverend Homer. I ought to hold you in contempt and throw you out of this case, Ridley. I'm not going to do it because I do not want a mistrial, but pull that kind of trick once more and I hold you in contempt and put you in a cell—you have my word on that."

7

WHEREVER THERE was a doorway, a hallway, an entrance, or an exit in the limited world of the trial, some part of the media gathered. If the most interesting thing in the country was happening in Clarkton, it was nevertheless a single event about which only so much could be written; thus the search to increase its complexity. When Jim Cooper, shortly after the court had closed for the day, appeared at the offices of the Ridleys with a small, stout bald man in tow, a shout went up for comment or statement. The man's name was Carl Haberman, and he had the reputation of being the best criminal lawyer in the East, with New York City as his base of operation.

"Are you joining the defense?"

"Did they hire you, Mr. Haberman?"

"What are Abigail's chances?"

Haberman said nothing. Jim Cooper informed them that there was a press conference scheduled for eight o'clock.

Abigail, Bill, the Ridleys, Rita Asbury, Allie Jones—all of them, defendant, lawyers, secretaries—all of them gathered in the front reception room and waited as Jim slipped into the office, herding the small fat man in front of him. He had telephoned them half an hour before, telling them that he was at the hotel with Carl Haberman, who had come unbidden from New York and insisted that he speak to them.

"All right, we'll talk to him," Jack had said.

Now they greeted him and introduced themselves and led him into the conference room, the secretaries with their pencils and pads ready.

"I'd like this off the record," Haberman said. "You're not running a tape, are you?"

"No, we have no tape in this office."

"I know that you and the Ridleys are determined to see this thing through on your own and without any outside help. I think it's a bad decision. Can you tell me why?"

"Because we decided that they got no law on their side," Jack Ridley said. "They got no law whatsoever, they're in violation of the state constitution and they're in violation of the Constitution of the United States. This is Bill and Abigail's position, and we agree with them. We fight this as ordinary citizens, not as distinguished counsel with a firm of two hundred lawyers."

"Forgive me, please, but that's the most foolish statement I have listened to these past many years."

"We didn't invite you here to insult us," Bill said.

"Forgive me. I'm a widower, but if I were married to a woman like Abigail here, I'd be thinking of only one thing—how to get her out of here alive. For God's sake, don't you realize what's happening? You talk about the Constitution—we have a new Supreme Court. There is no Constitution. Think about the Supreme Court and what you can expect from it. Don't you understand what is happening? Let me tell you that no state would indict on this crazy law unless Washington had given the nod. It's not abortion that's on trial here—it's women. Suppose women can swing the next election, take power in a new sense, a majority of women in both houses of the government—and even the possibility of an executive controlled by women. Do you know what we're moving into—the first real battle of the war against women. Abigail Goodman, test case. Let's try it on for size and see whether it fits." He looked around the table.

After a long moment of silence, Jack said, "I don't buy that. I just don't."

"Of course not. You're a man," Button said. "I buy it."

"It doesn't add up," Bill said.

"It makes a lot of sense to me," Abigail decided.

"I want to help," said Haberman.

"Mr. Haberman," Bill said, "we may be simplistic, but we saw

109

only two ways to fight this: to prove as well as we could with expert witnesses that Professor Goodman's abortion took place in the first trimester of her pregnancy, and that abortion is not murder, and second, to prove that an ex post facto law was in violation of the Constitution and of the essence of common law. We may not have found every citation and case in which ex post facto decisions were either rejected or overturned, but we have enough to make our case."

"It's more subtle than that," Haberman said.

"Of course it is. The constitution of this state says that a measure becomes law when passed by a majority of the two houses in the legislature. It also says that the governor has the right to veto the law during the two weeks after the legislature passes it. If he signs the law during that period, he is simply relinquishing his right to veto. In other states, it becomes law either when the governor signs it or if he lets a given period pass without signing. To all effects, it's the same thing. The state here argues that a bill becomes law when it is passed. We hold that it does not become law until the governor signs it. It is ambiguous, but we feel that we can fight through and win on that basis."

Haberman shook his head.

"Why not?" Bill demanded.

"Because on that point, considering that this trial is a show-case, you're in this state and this court. The judge will control it in his charge to the jury. You see, your case is not built on facts or evidence, it's built on interpretation, and that's a deadly mistake in a hostile state and a hostile court. You're forgetting that this is a trial—not an appeal."

A long silence hung over them after Haberman finished. Then Abigail said to him, "What would you do, Mr. Haberman?"

"What is a crime here is not a crime in Connecticut or New York or California. For example, adultery is still on the books of certain states as a crime, with severe penalties attached to it. Adultery in Saudi Arabia is a capital crime. The law has no resonance whatsoever in the United States. States have made flag burning a crime; other states have not. We argue that this law is meaningless in every other state and that this state indicts Professor Goodman in violation of all common law. We go into federal court with a false arrest and psychological damage suit against the State—I would say that one hundred million dollars would set them back on their heels. Not that it means much, but it's a part of a total aggressive stance. But you can't create this with the forces you have at your disposal. I want to bring in half a dozen of the best young lawyers in our firm. The law works two ways—don't ever forget that."

"You see, Mr. Haberman," Jack said, "my wife and I have been taking on civil rights cases since we began our practice. We were pretty damn successful, considering the state we live in."

"This is no civil rights case," Haberman said.

"Yes, I know. On the other hand—I guess we had enough faith in America—"

"Yes, Boy Scouts have faith in America."

Bill said, "You talk about taking on this case—well, we have had other offers, not with men of your reputation or caliber, but other offers, and for one reason or another, we turned them down. Now your offer, yourself and half a dozen lawyers from your firm—my God, Mr. Haberman, your price alone must be three, four hundred dollars an hour."

"Pro bono," Haberman said shortly.

"Why?"

"Because I love this country and I want to live here and I want my children and grandchildren to live here. Will you take me on?"

"I know we should be overwhelmed," Bill told him. "Why don't you sit in my office for a few minutes—we need to talk among ourselves."

Bill took Haberman to his office. When he returned to the conference room, the others were locked in heated debate.

"I could have been wrong," Abigail was saying. "After all, I think I talked you into it, and that we had to do it ourselves. It was the whole thing of the South and my grandfather, and the way the rest of the country looks at us—"

"And you had a point," Jack said. "A damn important point."

"But I'm not a lawyer," Abigail argued. "I read about the way they do these things in New York and Los Angeles, with their batteries of lawyers, and I've never understood—and anyway, it felt so wonderful in all this hideous nightmare that perhaps we could make something positive out of it, so that even if I lost—"

"We're not going to lose!" Bill snapped.

"The point is," Jack said, "that you've been watching this circus for days now."

"Yes."

"I was on your side, Abigail," Ridley said. "I had other reasons. I don't fall into that strike-a-blow-for-liberty pattern. Most of the blows for liberty are horseshit anyway."

"You're thinking that Haberman's Jewish, that they'll lock on to that," Bill said.

"Yes, that's what I'm thinking."

"It's already a fact with me, isn't it?"

"To some degree, Bill," Jack said.

"What the hell! At least he'll bring us a new angle and more experience than you and me put together. He makes us a pretty magnificent offer. Let's take him up on it."

"You know of course that we're absolutely crazy," Button said. "This smart little guy comes in and lays a million dollars' worth of the best law in the country on us, and we debate whether we accept. Have we lost our senses? We ought to get down on our knees and thank him. I am going to Mr. Haberman," Button snapped, "and I am going to thank him and bless him, and if you and Jack don't like that, Abigail and I will finish the trial with Haberman as our collaborating counsel."

July 17. Eileen Mott, special to the *New York Globe:*

Unobtrusively, without fanfare or public statement, Carl Haberman has slipped into Clarkton and closeted himself with the defense team in the trial of Professor Abigail Goodman. Whether he will join the defense team I do not know. The Goodman defense has been quite rigid about refusing the aid of distinguished counsel, even though a number of nationally known criminal lawyers have volunteered their services.

The interesting thing about Mr. Haberman is that he is not known as a criminal lawyer, even though there was national coverage of his defense of Gertrude Connolly. You will recall that Mrs. Connolly, a battered wife who had been hospitalized several times due to injuries inflicted by her husband, deliberately and carefully planned the murder of her husband. The murder was not in direct response to beating or threats, but calmly premeditated, eliminating any claim to self-defense. Carl Haberman stepped into her case and won her freedom.

Mr. Haberman's forte has been constitutional law, a field in which he is widely respected, and at one time there was talk of a possible nomination to the Supreme Court. In the case of *Associated Telephone* versus *National Telephone,* Mr. Haberman persisted in a legal battle that took seven years; and against all odds, he broke the hold of National Telephone. In the case of *Jones* versus *Federal Tobacco,* he won for his client a punitive award of thirty million dollars, the largest such award ever granted in a New York court.

In appearance, Carl Haberman is short and plump, thin hair, pink cheeks, and a pleasant smile—a mild and disarming appearance. However, I am told that he is a skilled litigator and prefers, at critical moments in a trial, to do his own litigation.

In college, Abigail had made world history her major and then had gone on to get a master's degree in European history. She decided to go for a doctorate and do a study of women's role in history. Marriage and children put a temporary halt to that. Abigail was determined to be a mother above other things, to be with her children, and to do what work she could at home. While Bill struggled with his law practice, Abigail raised the children, worked on her dissertation, and, eight years after she had begun, received her doctorate. After that, she wrote on the subject of women in history, made a reasonably solid name for herself in the field of women's rights, and convinced the people at Hilden College, a small but excellent Episcopal institution, to allow her to design a new course to be called "Women in History." Her two children were off to college, and after all the years of child raising and adolescent mediation, she was again a reasonably free woman.

In the first semester of her course, she had as students seventeen girls, three boys, and a constant flow of male and female faculty observers. She held back on none of her convictions and not only plunged into historical revision, but stood a great deal of history on its head. Momentarily, she expected to be interfered with, stopped, tossed out; but none of that happened. She was given a free hand, and as a Baptist turned agnostic married to a Jew, she emerged with a new respect for Episcopalians, at least in terms of Hilden College.

Life opened up for Abigail. Here she was, not yet forty-two and picking up on all the dreams she had abandoned two decades ago. She was teaching new material; every day was a challenge; she was earning a decent salary, and she had the feeling that she and Bill had stepped into an entirely new life. The trip from her home to the college was only a few miles, but it was being away and on her own that put the frosting on her feeling of emancipation.

And then, one day, reality reached out and touched her, and she said to Bill, "Do you know, I think I missed my period."

"Oh, come on." He was shaving at that moment, and she stood at the door to the bathroom, and he was watching her in the mirror, possibly thinking that he was a lucky man indeed to have this slender, attractive, and intelligent woman as his wife, possibly thinking that for the first time in years he was just jealous as hell about her consorting with that good-looking crowd at the college, and possibly thinking nothing very much except that here was his wife and a pleasant sight indeed.

"Well, how do you feel?"

"I feel wonderful."

"So forget it. You'll come around."

But she didn't come around, and one day she stopped in at the hospital, and the next day she said to Bill, "Honey, I'm pregnant."

"What!"

"Pregnant."

"Come on, you're kidding."

"Not about this," Abigail said.

"How do you know?"

"I stopped in at the hospital. I saw Dr. Masell," she said.

"What did he say?"

"I told you what he said," she answered testily. "He said that I'm pregnant. He examined me, and he said there's no reason why I can't have the child if I want to. He said that at my age the odds for a healthy birth might be a bit less than normal, but still and all, he said there was no real problem in that direction— maybe not as easy—"

"Well, you must have thought about it . . . ?"

"I've thought of nothing else, be sure of that."

"And?"

"Bill, I don't want to talk about it. Not right now. I told you because I felt that you should know."

"Thank you," he said shortly.

"Oh, for God's sake, don't get up on a high horse. I don't need that now. I'm shaken enough and troubled enough, so don't jump on me. Give me some space. Let me think about it."

"Oh, sure. Absolutely."

"And keep it to ourselves, please."

"Absolutely."

He moved to embrace her and kiss her, but it was the wrong moment. She pulled away and went upstairs to her room and sprawled out on the bed.

Bill, wisely, did not bring it up again, and Abigail came to it in her own good time. One day at breakfast, apropos of nothing that might provoke it, she began to cry. She did not cry easily, and some of their worst moments had not brought her to tears. Bill's concern, his nervous reaction, were provoked by anticipation of some dreadful announcement. Had a doctor told her she had an awful disease? Not the pregnancy. He had already decided that he would go along with any decision on her part and that it was her decision to make.

"I can't go through with it," Abigail said.

"No, I didn't think you would want to."

"Bill, I'm too old. I can't begin again. I love you and I love being your wife, but that isn't enough and I can't live with that, and I loved being a mother, but I can't do that again. This past year has been the best year of our marriage. You know that. I know it. I can't give it all up."

"No. I don't think you should."

"Honestly?"

"Honestly," he said.

"I'm not being selfish. We have good, decent children. My work is important. Why must I be denied the right to do it?"

"No one denies you that right."

"I suppose I could do it and fight my way through. But to what end?"

118

"Abigail, my dear, there is no onus attached to this. No guilt. Believe me, it is your body and your right to do with it as you decide."

"I can't tell you how torn I am," Abigail pleaded. "I've thought my way in and out of this a hundred times. I want to do it, but I can't. It's not only going through the pregnancy, it's having a child that I didn't want and trying to pretend otherwise. Well, I can't."

More or less, this was the story that Abigail spelled out to Haberman. She told it simply and directly, not trying to justify herself in any way and not in terms of any apology.

Haberman nodded. "Now that you have said all this, my dear, you will forget it."

"What do you mean? How can I forget it?"

"By not telling it to any other living soul. You are being tried for having an abortion, do you understand? Let us try to forget about right and wrong, just and unjust. Let us begin to think as lawyers think. Please," he said to Bill and the Ridleys, "forgive me for being didactic, but I have twenty years of teaching at Columbia University. It makes one didactic. You have all fallen into a pit. It is understandable. In your justified rage over this situation, you have answered their indictment with a counterindictment of the right to life philosophy. You counter their mistakes with your own mistakes. The State today used their witness to try to prove that abortion was murder—that's all. Not one word to the effect of whether or not an abortion ever took place."

"But they have the records from the hospital," Jack argued.

"Forget those records for the time being. Later, we will dis-

119

cuss the records from Hilden, but for the time being, forget them. Think about the indictment. Abortion is not on trial. Abigail Goodman is on trial. Have they called any witness to testify about the alleged abortion?"

"No, of course not," Bill said. "Our strategy will be to prove that an abortion cannot be classified as murder, and that thereby my wife has committed no crime."

"But the new law says that abortion is murder," Haberman said gently. "Abigail is being tried for violation of a law. The charge against Abigail is abortion. Don't you understand? They must prove that an abortion took place—"

"Right on!" Button exploded.

"The evidence from Hilden," Jack began, "cannot be—"

"Forget it, please," Haberman said. "They have fallen into a trap, out of stupidity and arrogance. Leave them there. Not a word from us about the fact that they are presenting no witness who will testify to the abortion itself. We don't even whisper what I am saying here. We pray that they will continue in the same mode. On the other hand, Abigail, not one word of admission to the abortion. There was no abortion."

"But there was."

"And they must prove it."

"Do you understand, Abby?" Button said. "They are presenting the wrong body of proof. I think I know why. They feel the question of whether the abortion took place has been settled. That's why they arrested you. They had the evidence from Hilden, and they decided that was all they required. I suppose this lousy governor of ours said, 'You've got the proof. Now make a showcase of this. Prove to the world that our position on abortion is right, moral, religious—whatever.' "

"And we do not shake the cart," Haberman said softly. "In the cross-examination of the State's witnesses, we play their game. We do not even whisper the question of guilt or innocence in the matter of an alleged crime."

July 17. Moshe Katz, special to *Ha Shem,* Tel Aviv:

Carl Haberman, the famous constitutional lawyer, internationally known for his long battle against the Federal Tobacco Company and for the enormous punitive damages awarded his client at the time, thirty million dollars, has apparently joined the Abigail Goodman defense team. As far as we can learn, his services are being delivered pro bono, in American legal terminology, without payment. Since we have been told that he intends to bring at least six of his associates into the case, the gift to the defense is quite substantial—a legal gift that might, under other circumstances, amount to over a million dollars.

When pressed to explain his action, Mr. Haberman said, "This is a case that will make law, and I don't know a lawyer who would not want to get into something that will make law. Or unmake it, as we hope, for here we are dealing with a law so malignant and threatening that it defies civilization. But even such extreme measures are not without precedent, nor are ex post facto laws without precedent. But in almost every case they have been repealed or overthrown by a higher court. We are going to fight very hard, and we are not without weapons."

When asked whether this meant that he would depend on appeal to a higher court if defeated here in Clarkton, Mr. Haberman replied that they would certainly appeal as high as the Supreme Court of the United States—a move that is questionable in the light of the Supreme Court's abandonment of *Roe* versus *Wade*. Being faced, as we are here in Israel, with the right-wing orthodoxy's campaign against abortion, this case is of particular interest to Israeli citizens.

One cannot spend even a few days here in Clarkton, USA, without sensing another factor that has entered into this case: anti-Semitism. There is a curious kind of anti-Semitism that appears to take flower in the most backward parts of this country. Those of my readers who are at all familiar with Jewish history in America will remember the Leo Frank case. Leo Frank came of a German-Jewish family. He was born in Cuero, Texas, in 1884. He studied mechanical engineering and on invitation of his uncle, Moses Frank, owner of a pencil factory in Atlanta, Georgia, moved to that city and took on the job of plant manager for the pencil factory.

In April of 1913, a fourteen-year-old girl, Mary Phagan by name, an employee at the pencil factory, was found murdered in the basement. On trumped-up charges that had little foundation, Leo Frank was arrested, charged with the murder, and convicted on perjured evidence. When Governor John Slaton commuted Frank's death sentence to life imprisonment, Tom Watson, a southern Populist politician who gained fame for his racism and who delivered it in a weekly magazine he owned called the *Jefferson Weekly,* began a deadly campaign against Leo Frank, whom he characterized as "the filthy, perverted Jew of New York." As a result of this and Watson's tireless campaign against Jews, a lynch mob broke into the jail where Frank was held, dragged him out, and lynched him.

I could not help recalling these events after a few days in Clarkton. Twice the local paper made mention of the fact that William Goodman, husband of Abigail Goodman, was a Jew, born and raised in New York City, and a graduate of Harvard Law School. There has been innuendo concerning the corruption of an old southern line, the Hendersons, through marriage to the New York Jew, and in today's local paper, Carl Haberman was characterized as the "New York Jew lawyer." The subtlety of this kind of slur is difficult to explain in translation, but in English, Jew is the noun, whereas Jewish is the adjective. Normally, the adjective would define the noun, but by the substitution of the noun for the adjective, Jew for Jewish, a subtle but vicious insult is perpetrated. When I took this up with Jack Ridley, chief of the defense team and a Clarkton native, he spoke of his own anger and said he had already taken it up with the editor of the newspaper. "But we can do nothing about it," he explained. "They can print anything they please."

On the other hand, one of the State's witnesses will be a New York City Orthodox rabbi, Herschel Cohen by name, who, I am told, has supported the Right to Life groups—that is, the anti-abortion people. This maneuver is evidently calculated to counter any charge of officially inspired anti-Semitism.

As a footnote to what I have just written, I must mention that at the United Nations in New York, a great international conference on the future of the planet Earth has just convened. Professor Ramu Chatterjee of Calcutta University delivered a paper on overpopulation, rejecting the charge that only India and China threaten life on the planet through excess population—in other words, more people than the planet can sustain. Professor Chatterjee offered evidence to demonstrate that an American family with just two children, but with an automobile, refrigerator, lawn mower, electric power, and air-conditioning plus oil heat, does more to pollute the planet than eighty Indian peasants.

In the light of this, the local obsession with Right to Life, as the anti-abortionists call themselves, is mind-boggling. One begins to feel, here in Clarkton, that all recourse to sanity has gone by the board.

8

July 18. Bosley Kent, Reuters:

An extraordinary set of events were reported today on the front page of *The Clarion,* the major newspaper in this state's capital. Abortion has been illegal in this state for seventeen years, but after the original decision by the United States Supreme Court in the case of *Roe* versus *Wade,* the enforcement of local laws has been desultory and intermittent. Now with *Roe* versus *Wade* robbed of its teeth and with the passage by the state legislature of section 157, making abortion punishable by death, the situation has changed abruptly.

According to *The Clarion,* a series of police raids were

undertaken yesterday in the state capital, and 37 illegal abortionists were arrested. Of these, 12 were physicians. Along with them, 16 women in the process of undergoing abortions were arrested. The records taken by the police furnish the names of 193 women who have undergone abortions since the passage of 157. Of course, it is still to be determined how many of these abortions were done after the first trimester of the pregnant women concerned.

The story in *The Clarion* states that all 37 of the illegal abortionists, the physicians included, are being held without bail, under indictments charging them with premeditated murder. How many of their patients will be similarly charged remains to be seen: But in speaking to some of the other correspondents covering the Abigail Goodman trial here in Clarkton, I got the impression that things are on the edge of getting completely out of hand.

Bills similar to the famous—or infamous, depending upon one's point of view—section 157 have been introduced or are in the process of being introduced in nine other states of the Union. Each of these nine states has a politically active Right to Life movement and possibly a Right to Life majority among the voters. Nevertheless, the explosive expansion of what started in Clarkton with the indictment of Professor Abigail Goodman has aroused fear and anger among millions of Americans. Congress is engaged in a bitter debate on the question of a bill duplicating the content of *Roe* versus *Wade,* and even the White House has given indications of feeling that the matter of section 157 has gone too far.

Meanwhile, here in Clarkton, the trial of Professor Good-
man goes on. Both Abigail Goodman and her husband, William
Goodman, present a calm and frequently cheerful public face.
They reiterate their belief that they will win in this trial.

To find an unoccupied hotel room in Clarkton was impossible. Every motel and bed & breakfast was occupied, and people
were renting out their campers. Fortunately for Haberman,
some distant relatives of his had a haberdashery in town. Their
name was Klein, and when they heard that their famous second
cousin was coming to town—news from his office, with a plea
that he might stay with them—they were only too delighted.

In the car, driving to the house of this cousin, Haberman
asked Bill about Freda Swanson.

"Planned Parenthood in Connecticut. She's one of those extraordinary women who seems able to get almost anything done.
She's been down here for weeks now."

"Amazing woman," Haberman said. "Everything I used to
think I knew about women is spinning around in my head. My
wife died of cancer two years ago. I'd give my right arm to be
able to spend a year with my wife again."

The Klein house was on a small, quiet street. Their children
were grown and out of the house, so a spare room for Haberman was not a problem.

"They can't seem to come to grips with what is happening

here. They kept asking me about the Leo Frank case," Haberman said. "The case of a factory manager in Atlanta who was falsely accused of the murder of one of the factory girls, tried, and then lynched by a mob. That was many years ago—"

"I've heard of it," Abigail said quietly. "I know the story only too well."

"My cousin took his basic training in a military camp near here. He was nineteen when he came out of the service after World War Two. He came back here to open a men's clothing store and married a local girl. Now both of them are very frightened."

"What do you think?" Bill asked her after they had dropped off Haberman at the Klein home.

"He's a nice little man, sensitive, smart—I think he's very smart. I don't understand why he's doing this. Do you?"

"Sort of."

"Tell me."

"I can feel it—I don't know whether I can explain it. His being Jewish has something to do with it."

"Because you're Jewish?"

"No. I'm sure he'd act the same way whether I was Protestant or Catholic. I suppose it's a burden he carries, but that doesn't explain it, either. I mean his being Jewish, not me. Do you understand?"

"Not really, no."

But there was a great deal Abigail did not understand, not simply the role of Haberman, but the sense she had of forces moving around her, using her. She thought about the stories she remembered of witches bound to the stake and burned; the auto-da-fé, the act of faith in the time of the Spanish Inquisition. But these people were not witches. Here was a new act of madness, the act of a world torn loose from sanity and common sense.

She resented and disliked the need to live in a hotel room. This room had been their home for weeks now, the bad pictures on the walls, the cheap carpet on the floor, the dry, chitinous smell of the place, the yellow light oozing out of low-voltage bulbs, the wretched little stand she tried to use as a dressing table.

"God, I'm tired," Bill said. He was reading the telephone messages that had been slid under the door. "The kids. They called twice today."

"They caught me at the office," Abigail said. "They want so desperately to come down here, to be with us, to support me. I told Leon flat out that the only thing he and Hope could do for me is to stay away. If they were here, I'd be so sick with worry and fear, I couldn't go on. Don't you see"—her tone became more strident, more desperate—"don't you see what could happen? If anything happened to them—"

She sat loosely now, passive. "It's not any good. They call it air-conditioning, but it's not any good. It's so wet and miserable."

After she had showered, she felt a little better, almost relaxed. Bill was already in bed, the covers turned down for her. She sat on the edge of the bed and said, almost wanly, "Billy dear, please make love to me tonight, please."

He looked at her with a sort of amazement.

"You haven't touched me—no, you haven't made love to me since we're down here. Do you remember when Maude Kellogg had her mastectomy? She told me Al wouldn't go near her for weeks. Billy, don't you understand?"

He put his arms around her and held her.

"Make love to me, please."

July 19. Conte Laponi, special to *Avanti:*

The second witness called today in the trial of Professor Abigail Goodman, under the strange new law in the United States that calls for the death sentence for abortion, is Bishop Collins, a Catholic priest. It would appear, at least from the treatment of the first witness, Dr. Joseph Lang, that there will be few opportunities for correspondents to question and interview the witnesses. They are carefully sequestered and guarded as they are escorted into the courthouse and out of it, and arrangements have been made to quarter them apart from the town itself, in what is called a motor court here locally.

My own good fortune, speaking journalistically, was to encounter Father Collins in a small, special men's room—to which I was ushered, the main bathroom being fully occupied, by a kindly court attendant who recognized my extreme need. Father Collins occupied the adjoining urinal, and having gotten over

my childhood belief that priests, kings, queens, and other ex-
alted beings neither defecated nor urinated, and having guessed
that the reversed collar worn by this tall, lean, and serious gentleman was more likely to belong to the forthcoming witness
than any local clergyman who had wandered into this VIP toilet
by mistake, I informed the good father, speaking very rapidly,
that I was an Italian newspaperman, and that since I came from
an almost entirely Catholic country, my readers would be in-
tensely interested in any statement he decided to make.

My accent may have intrigued him. He said if I could de-
vise a question in the time it took for him to zipper his pants and
button his waistcoat, he might be tempted to answer it. If he had
given me a little more time, I might have devised something
clever and important, but since he had already zippered up and
was in the process of buttoning his waistcoat, I simply blurted
out, "Where is charity and mercy if a priest stands as a witness
for this prosecution?"

He finished buttoning his vest but did not depart. "You are
not a Catholic?" he said.

"I was born and baptized a Catholic. I don't go to church,
and I haven't been to confession in twenty years."

"And you talk about mercy?"

"I didn't know that one depended on the other."

"More's the pity," he said, and left the room and left me
feeling like a fool, a feeling not unfamiliar to me, recalling the
priests and nuns of my school days.

I will have more to say about Father Collins, I trust, after
listening to his testimony. I must add, however, that I feel totally

mired, even suffocated, by what is happening here in this town. My British and American colleagues seem to be taking it in their stride, accepting it as another one of the series of apparently endless puritanical lunacies that seem to have marked their civilization since it began. I am afraid I cannot look upon it in that easy manner. To me, it is the beginning of something dark and ugly that chills my blood as few things have since the distant days of Benito Mussolini and Adolf Hitler.

9

Bishop Frank Collins was not one of your laid-back, stout, easygoing priests, not one to put love before sin in any order of importance; he was tall, lean, and handsome, with dark eyes almost black and that hawklike look of the western Irish counties. He did not fuss or flutter with his answers but came down hard and right to the point, as when Anderson asked him whether he could say what, in his faith, was understood to be sin.

Ridley objected, but the judge allowed the question to stand, and Haberman, who had been admitted into the defense that morning, whispered to Ridley, "This is a sly one. Careful."

"I have made this objection before," Ridley said. "I make it again. This puts a religious cloak on what is a case in law. My client is charged with a crime. Whether or not the action for which she is being tried is sinful is simply not pertinent." He contained himself as he finished.

Anderson argued, "If one burns down a church or a synagogue, that is a criminal act, but a religious act as well. Would you deny a rabbi's testimony on the burning of a synagogue, if the arsonist argues that it is not a religious matter?"

"We are not dealing with the burning of a synagogue or a church!" Jack argued hotly. "What kind of nonsense is this? We are not even dealing with sin, when you come down to it. We are in a court of law dealing with law. My client is not being charged with sin or accused of being a sinner."

"Of course she is," Anderson snorted.

"She is accused of breaking the law, not sinning."

"And that constitutes a sin!"

"Mr. Anderson," the judge said sharply, "I must remind you again that this is a courtroom, not a church. We are trying a violation of section 157 of this state's criminal code. Try to remember that. As for the question of sin, it relates to the training and judgment of the witness. I am going to allow him to answer the question."

"Then I take exception, and I want my exception on the record," Ridley said.

"So noted," Benson said. "The question is allowed."

"Would you answer the question, Bishop Collins?" Anderson said.

"Of course. I would begin by quoting St. Augustine, namely, 'Sin is a word, a deed, or a desire in opposition to the eternal law.' We interpret this by regarding a sinful act or thought as a deliberate transgression of the law of God. The law of God tells us that there are four essentials to every sin. We divide laws into two categories. There are the physical laws, whose function is derived out of necessity, but there are also moral laws, which apply to human beings. Sin is a transgression of moral law, and thereby is offensive to God. Will you say that the Divine Will cannot be disobeyed? But Catholicism holds that grace can be resisted, and thereby the Divine Will is disobeyed. Such transgression is deliberate, since the sinner always knows that he acts contrary to the laws of God."

"Thank you, Bishop Collins. Now as to abortion, does the Church regard it as a sin?"

"It does."

"In what way, sir?"

Jack objected again but was overruled.

"We recognize two categories of sin," the bishop said.

"We. By we, I presume you mean your church?"

"Exactly. I must remind the court that all sin is an offense against God, but venial sin is forgivable. That is, venial sin does not involve the loss of grace. Mortal sin destroys sanctifying grace and brings about the supernatural death of the soul."

"I see. And how does your church regard abortion?"

"As mortal sin."

"The death of the sinner's soul?"

Ridley was on his feet, objecting angrily. "This calls not only for a conclusion, but for a theological conclusion that has absolutely nothing to do with this case. In fact, this man's entire testimony has nothing to do with this case. Mrs. Goodman is not on trial for sinning. She is charged with having an abortion. I ask for all of his testimony to be stricken."

"You are overruled," Benson said.

"I ask for an exception."

"So noted." The judge directed a finger at Anderson. "The bishop, sir, is your witness, a friendly witness. Try to hold him to the case in point."

Anderson shrugged, turned to the jury, allowed a thin smile to slide onto his face, corrected it, sighed, turned to the judge, and said, "I have no more for this witness."

"Your witness, Mr. Ridley," the judge said.

"I am a Baptist, Bishop Collins," Jack said flatly. "Am I a sinner?"

"I can't answer that," the bishop said.

"Am I in a state of grace?"

"I would hesitate to condemn you."

"I'm not in a confession booth, Bishop. I am in an American courtroom. I simply asked whether I am in a state of grace or in a state of sin."

"It is impossible for me to answer that question."

"It should be equally impossible for him to ask that question!" Anderson declared triumphantly, leaping to his feet. "He just lectured the jury on the fact that we are not, to use his words, dealing with sin, but with law and the violation of the law. But now he demands of Bishop Collins whether he is in sin? I mean Mr. Ridley. I do not mean Bishop Collins."

"Mr. Anderson," the judge said quietly.

"Your Honor."

"Mr. Anderson, I happen to occupy the bench in this case. I am wide awake, and I am capable of following this trial, and I am even capable of remembering prior testimony. A simple objection is sufficient, and you may trust me to know the law or lack of law behind your objection. Try to remember that when you open a door, you cannot close it because you dislike the wind. If your speech is an objection, I deny it."

He turned to Ridley. "Go on, Mr. Ridley."

"Bishop Collins, speaking as a Baptist, I must remind you that there are thirty-three million of us, worldwide. Are we all sinners according to your lights?"

Anderson rose to object, and the judge said, "Enough! As I said, you opened this, so let's get on with it."

"Would you please answer the question, Bishop!"

"It is not within my province to say."

"A vote on choice as opposed to right to life was taken in four Baptist congregations in California. Choice won out, sixty percent to forty percent. Are these sixty percent Baptists in mortal sin?"

"I told you that this is not in my province."

"What is the meaning of Catholic?"

"Its lay meaning is universal," the bishop said, showing annoyance for the first time. "But today the term is used in reference to Christians who hold to a continuing tradition of faith and worship and who hold to the apostolic succession of bishops and priests since the time of Christ."

"But you will make no comment on Baptists?"

"No, sir. As I said, that is not my province."

"And if a Baptist should practice abortion, would the doctor who performed the abortion and the woman whose embryo is aborted go straight to hell?"

For the first time, the bishop hesitated. But only for an instant, and then, smiling, he answered, "Only after death, I think."

The press box burst into laughter, jury and audience joining them. Benson banged his gavel for order. Jack bowed in appreciation.

"I am pleased to find that you have a sense of humor, Bishop, but you also leave me somewhat disturbed. Doing a quick bit of loose arithmetic, I come up with five or six million Baptists bound straight for hell. Since my mommy and daddy were good churchgoing Baptists and just about the best people I ever knew and loved, and since I have found that to be the case with any number of other Baptists I have come across, nice folk, sir, it pains me that so many of them are damned—according to what you say."

Benson said, "You are not making your closing remarks, Mr. Ridley. I suggest that instead of lecturing the witness, you question him, and if you have a question, get to it!"

"I was on my way, Your Honor, but shaken by a fate that might befall so many good churchgoing Baptists."

The audience broke into laughter again, and Benson banged

with his gavel. "I will not have that in this court. This is a deadly serious trial, not a sideshow."

Jack Ridley apologized. "I understand that, Your Honor. But it is also a trial without precedent in my experience."

"Go on with your cross-examination," the judge said.

"An exit poll at a large Catholic church in Chicago showed that twenty-two percent of the congregation favored choice. Does that consign them to hell?"

"I certainly would not," the bishop replied, "but I don't sit in judgment. Perhaps if I heard their confessions—"

"You spoke of the immortal soul before. This is the property of every human being, is it not?"

"Yes, it is."

"And when does this immortal soul appear in the human being? At birth?"

"Oh, no! No indeed!" the bishop said emphatically. "It appears at the moment of conception—as a gift of God."

"I see. How do you know this, Bishop?"

"It is an article of my faith."

"Oh? Well, sir, I was baptized here in Clarkton, total immersion, and I went to an excellent church Sunday school. I accepted the fact that people have immortal souls. But I was never told that this soul appeared at the moment of conception. How do you account for such oversight? Is it a built-in failing of Baptists?"

"I will not comment on that."

"But you are so certain. Why won't you comment?"

"It is not my province."

"Well," Ridley said, turning to the jury, "I certainly do hope you can explain to God where the borders of your province are, since I can't make head or tail of said borders."

Anderson was on his feet, shouting, and the judge turned angrily to Ridley. "I won't have that, Mr. Ridley. You know exactly what I mean."

Jack apologized. "Let us get back to the question of the immortal soul," he said, quietly now. "I recall asking our pastor, Warren Deats, about the immortal soul. I was twelve years old, if I remember rightly, and at that age one tends to get nervous about growing up and dying—"

"Mr. Ridley," the judge interrupted.

"I am framing my question, Your Honor. Well, Pastor Deats took a practical approach. He said that if I stopped sneaking smokes and thought less about girls and didn't lie to my momma and daddy, then it would do more for my immortal soul than any explanation he could provide—"

"Mr. Ridley!"

"Yes, Your Honor. I'm at the question. I am quoting Father John A. Hardon, Society of Jesus"—he turned to the jury—"Jesuit, a large, important, and highly intellectual section of the Catholic church. Father Hardon is an esteemed theologian of the Catholic church." He turned back to the bishop now. "Quote: 'As a simple and spiritual substance, the soul cannot die, since a human person is composed of body animated by the soul.'" He paused. "Do you recognize the quotation, Bishop?"

"Yes."

"Have I quoted correctly, exactly, precisely?"

"As far as my recollection goes, yes. May I also add that you have quoted out of context."

"Yes, but isn't any religious quotation out of context? A religion is the whole life and thinking of a person—or at least so it is said to be."

"Yes, I would grant that."

"Now, Father Hardon says that a human being is composed of a body animated by a soul. Is there a soul without a body?"

"Yes, since the soul resides in God. And you will admit, sir," the bishop continued, "that Father Hardon also states that the soul appears at conception."

"So he does, but you will grant that in both cases, this is only a theological opinion of the Catholic church."

"Divinely inspired."

"But, Bishop, having been driven as a child to read the four Gospels and the Epistles as well and to memorize parts and to read them over and over, I still cannot recall any reference to the soul at the moment of conception. Insofar as I was taught Christianity, admitting that this was Baptist teaching, salvation and grace were of deeds, not a given."

"I cannot comment on Baptist teaching," the bishop said.

"Now, Bishop Collins, if the soul appears at the moment of fertilization, or conception if you prefer the term, the fertilized egg must then travel through the fallopian tube and up to the uterus. Now since you state that the soul appears at the moment of conception, granting that the universe is wired in some way for this to happen, then tell me what happens in the case of twins? In such a case, the fertilized egg splits into two in the

141

woman's tube. How then? Where are we now? Do we have one twin with a soul and one without a soul?"

"The Divine Spirit has taken this into consideration."

"How? When? When you speak of the Divine Spirit, do you mean God?"

"God the Father, and the Holy Spirit."

"And at that moment of conception, does the Holy Spirit split the soul, or are two souls provided?"

"If two souls are needed, God provides."

"I see." Ridley nodded. "I mention that I was raised a Baptist. My wife and law partner was raised an Episcopalian, which accounts for my interest in reading St. Augustine. She brought it with her, and I can't stand for her to have anything on her night table that I haven't read. Now, from my reading of St. Augustine, I find that he rejects the notion of a soul and a human being appearing at the moment of conception. Is that not so?"

"Yes, but—"

"That will do. A yes or no answer is sufficient. And is it not true that this teaching of St. Augustine was altered in the Middle Ages, the time in civilization's development when superstition ran rampant, in the Church and out of the Church?"

"I cannot—"

"I asked you whether St. Augustine's teaching was amended in the Middle Ages. Will you please answer yes or no."

"I am unable to answer that question."

Benson leaned over toward the bishop and said, "I think you can answer it, Bishop. It does come within your province."

"Yes," the bishop said sourly. "St. Augustine's teachings were amended."

"Thank you. Now tell me, Bishop Collins, do you know the meaning of in vitro as applied to the fertilization of a human egg cell?"

"I do."

Ridley turned to the judge and said, "Permit me, Your Honor, to explain the process to the jury?"

"Go ahead," Benson agreed.

"Ladies and gentlemen," he said to the jury, "there are women who desperately desire children, but for one reason or another are unable to conceive, either through a husband's difficulty or through some organic difficulty of their own. It was to help such women toward childbirth that science provided a solution. The woman's egg cell is removed from her body, placed in a dish, and fertilized with the man's sperm. Once the fertilization has taken place and is secure, the fertilized egg is returned to the body of the woman. This is what we call *in vitro.*"

He turned back to the bishop. "Sir, when that egg and sperm sits in its ceramic dish, does it have a soul?"

"If God wills."

"Yes, and I can tell you that the world will cease to be in sixty seconds if God wills it, and since the world continues to exist, I can hold that I know God's will. But I do not, and no human being does. Now please tell me whether that fertilized egg in the ceramic dish has a soul?"

"I must say that it has."

"And if someone tosses that dish into the sink, is that person guilty of murder?"

"By strict construction, I must say that he is."

"And what happens to that soul?"

"It returns to God."

"And suppose that in the course of developing this method which has brought children and happiness to so many human beings, the scientist at work fertilizes an egg experimentally, does that egg have a soul?"

"I must answer as I did before, yes."

"And let us suppose that in the course of developing this method of conception, the scientist must toss aside a dozen fertilized eggs. Does the whole dozen have souls?"

"Yes."

"Then each time he engages in work that has brought so much happiness to childless people, each time he brought his experiment along, he committed numerous acts of murder. Is this not so?"

"You are twisting my words out of context."

"How so?"

"When I spoke of the destruction of the fetus as an act of murder, I was talking about a deliberate action taken to prevent birth."

"Yes. But weren't you just as certain that at the instant the egg is fertilized, a soul comes into being, and that this soul is essentially a human being?"

"Yes," the bishop said.

"Ah!" Ridley turned back to the jury box, leaned upon the rail there, and asked the jury, "Isn't it wonderful how rhetoric can adjust to a situation?"

"Mr. Ridley!" the judge snapped. "I want no more of that!"

"I am sorry, Your Honor. Bishop, in your faith, is a murderer condemned to burn in hell forever?"

"Well, that's putting it dramatically. No. There is forgiveness even for murder. God's mercy has no limits. An act of contrition is meaningful."

"So there is a possibility that the scientist who had to destroy a dozen fertilized eggs could be forgiven for his murderous action, providing he made an act of contrition?"

"You are making a joke out of a very serious matter."

"No, sir," Jack cried. "I am not making a joke out of anything. I don't consider it a joke that a fine and loving woman is on trial for her life, accused of having an abortion. I ask you serious questions, and I base my questions on your own answers. Tell me, Bishop, what if this scientist were a Baptist and was totally unaware of the practice or meaning of an act of contrition? Would he burn in hell?"

"God would understand."

"Ah, yes," Jack said, walking back to the defense table and picking up a yellow pad. "You sit in that chair as an expert witness on abortion, but whenever your expertise is called upon, you let God sit in for you."

Anderson rose to object and to demand that Ridley show some respect and stop insulting his witness. "This is Bishop Collins, sir!" Anderson cried, feeling that the occasion called for a violation of the judge's instructions. "This is a holy man of the church. How dare you talk to him in this fashion! How dare you take the name of the Almighty in vain! You are badgering this man of God!"

Benson said, "Mr. Ridley, I know you understand the conduct of a trial and the laws of evidence. If I am called upon to chastise you again, it will not be to your advantage."

"I apologize."

The judge instructed the jury to disregard the last remarks of Mr. Ridley. Then Jack asked the bishop whether he knew what ectopic pregnancy was.

"I do."

"An ectopic pregnancy," Jack told the jury, "is a condition where the growth of the embryo takes place in the fallopian tubes instead of in the womb."

And turning to the bishop, "In that case, sir, the pregnant woman faces a choice between surgical abortion or death. How would you advise such a woman?"

Anderson was on his feet, objecting. "It calls for a conclusion."

"I'll rephrase," Jack agreed. "Is such an abortion an act of murder?"

"Obviously not!" the bishop exclaimed. "And I would ask you, sir, not to treat me as if I were some mindless witch doctor. Mine is an ancient and splendid faith, and if we have other ways than yours, try to understand, just as we have forbearance for your ways."

"My own apologies, Bishop Collins," Jack said. "I pride myself on the fact that I have never slighted or traduced the religion of another man, and I have the utmost respect for the antiquity and traditions of your church. However, is it not true that many thousands of devout Catholics call themselves the "underground church" and the "liberation church," and that these groups overwhelmingly support choice?"

"I have no statistics to bear out your statement."

"I see. Now in answer to an inquiry we put to Yale University Hospital in New Haven, we are told that they estimate that about twenty percent of all fertilized egg cells are lost through a more or less natural system. Now if you claim that each and every one of these millions of lost fertilized eggs contains a human soul, and that the doing away of these embryos after conception is an act of murder—"

"I make no such claim!" the bishop replied with annoyance.

"Of course not. You are a priest, a man of intelligence and compassion. And of course you don't believe that a scientist who experiments with a fertilized egg is guilty of murder. Do you?"

"Well, sir—"

"Please answer yes or no!" Jack insisted.

"No, I do not."

"Thank you, sir." Jack walked to the defense table, riffled through some papers, and then found what he wanted. He handed the sheet of paper to Judge Benson. "I would like this to be entered as evidence."

Benson scanned the sheet of paper and then handed it to Anderson, who had approached the bench.

"So be it," Benson said.

"Your Honor," Anderson said, "I must object to this," waving the sheet of paper. "I cannot imagine what Mr. Ridley is up to. This has absolutely no connection with the indictment or anything else relevant to this trial."

"Well, sir," the judge said, "there are more things relevant to this trial than you might imagine. I suppose Mr. Ridley proposes to connect it. Is that the case, Mr. Ridley?"

"Yes, Your Honor."

"Let's wait and see, Mr. Anderson. Hand it to the clerk, please."

Anderson handed the sheet of paper to the clerk, who marked it as evidence and then returned it to Jack Ridley, who handed it to Bishop Collins. "Take a moment to look through it, Bishop." Ridley walked to the jury box, then turned to face the bishop.

"Do you recognize it, sir?"

"Yes."

"Would you tell the jury what it is."

"It's apparently a photocopy of a story that appeared in *The New York Times* some time ago."

"You say apparently?"

"No, this is the story."

"Now, in the passage which we underlined in red ink, you are quoted. Do you feel, Bishop, that you were quoted correctly?"

"I think so. It was quite a long time ago, but I can remember even at that time feeling it was a correct quotation."

"Good. Now could I ask you to please read the underlined quotation to the jury."

"Oh, no. I must object most strongly," Anderson said, leaping to his feet. "What has this to do with this trial? How does it comport as evidence? I see no suggestion of evidence or of any connection. I object to Mr. Ridley's use of this courtroom to ride his political horses!"

"You know, Mr. Ridley, Mr. Anderson has a point," Judge Benson said. "Can you offer any reason why I should not sustain his objections?"

"Only my word that this will connect meaningfully. Your Honor, I am engaged in a cross-examination of the State's witness. If his own words either clarify or refute his present testimony, they are admissible. For him to admit under oath that this quotation I have asked him to read is in his own words removes any taint of hearsay."

Benson studied Ridley thoughtfully for a long moment, and then he said, "Very well, I will go along with you. I am going to deny the objections." He turned to the bishop. "Bishop Collins, will you please read aloud the quotation which you accepted as your own true statement."

The bishop then read, "The unspeakable murder of five Jesuit priests, following so hard upon the murder of the nuns and church workers and the murder of the presiding bishop in this community, is unlike any happening anywhere on earth. Almost seventy thousand people have been murdered by the death squads in this tiny country of El Salvador. The murder of any human being is horrible. There is no justification and there can be no justification for putting a human being to death."

"Thank you, Bishop Collins. However, in spite of the statement you have just read, you agreed to come here and bear witness to an accusation that if proven could result in the death of Abigail Goodman. Is that not so?"

"No, sir. That is not so. I am not here to bolster any verdict that will result in the death of Abigail Goodman."

"Then why are you here, sir?" Jack demanded harshly, approaching the bishop.

"To give the position of my church on abortion. Only that, sir. Nothing else."

"Really, Bishop? Do you see it that way? Nothing else?"

"Nothing else."

"Honestly put," Jack said. "You were introduced here on this witness stand by Mr. Anderson as a prosecution witness to an alleged abortion. Mr. Anderson questioned you about sin and abortion in terms of your competence, and he left it at that. All my questions to you were in terms of your expertise as a witness on sin, but you must understand that Mrs. Goodman is not accused of sinning. Is that not so?"

"I don't understand," the bishop said.

"Sinning, in large measure, Bishop Collins, is not against the law—that is, the state's law. Professor Goodman is not charged with sinning, but with abortion. Do you understand?"

"Yes, I do."

"Were you a witness to this alleged abortion?"

"No. Certainly not."

"Have you spoken to anyone who was witness to it?"

"No."

"Then how do you know that Professor Goodman ever had an abortion?"

"I was told so by Mr. Anderson."

"I see. And what evidence of this did he present to you?" Jack asked.

"His word—and of course the indictment."

"Only that?"

"Only that."

"I see." Jack nodded. Then he walked slowly to the jury box. He appeared to be lost in thought.

"He has it," Bill whispered to Button. "Why doesn't he let go?"

"Jack is sneaky. He can't bear to let go. He's pushed the bishop into defending the faith, and he's trying to figure out some way to use it."

"He was awfully good," Abigail said.

"Jack's good."

The judge said, "Mr. Ridley, are you finished with the witness?"

"Just another question or two."

"Then get on with it."

Suddenly Jack turned to the bishop and said, "What does Christianity mean to you, sir?"

Anderson was on his feet. "Oh, no! No way! This is too much."

"You have an objection?"

"Oh, absolutely."

"I will sustain it." Benson stared at Jack. "This is a very unusual trial, Mr. Ridley, yet for all of that, a very simple one. The indictment poses two questions: Has Mrs. Goodman had an abortion, and how far into her pregnancy did the abortion take place? That is all. That is what we are trying to prove here in court, but because of the very new and unprecedented elements in this case, I have given Mr. Anderson every liberty and I have given you every liberty. You have abused my willingness to be fair-minded."

"Your Honor," Jack said humbly, "I have put no witnesses in the box. These are Mr. Anderson's witnesses."

"Up here," the judge said. "Approach." When the two stood before him, he said softly, "You will make your own closing, Ridley. The bishop will not make it for you. This is becoming a damn circus, and I will not have it. Your stupid tricks are insulting. You want this witness to tell the jury that Christianity is compassionate and forgiving. Forget it."

Jack nodded. Anderson smiled thinly. Ridley then turned to the bishop and said, "I thank you for your compassionate and forgiving testimony. That's all. I have no other questions." Jack then walked back to the table, eyes downcast, avoiding any possibility of meeting Benson's gaze.

July 19. Julia Hyde, City Press Syndicate:

Today, Bishop Frank Collins took the stand for the prosecution in the trial of Professor Abigail Goodman. It is interesting that the State chose Bishop Collins as a witness for the official Catholic position, since in other political questions facing the Church, as for example the situation in El Salvador, where not only nuns and priests have been murdered by right-wing death squads but also a bishop of the Church, Father Collins's position has been squarely with the priests who supported the rebels against the death squads. However, so bizarre are the circumstances here that it is understandable that the State should seek for propriety to balance the extremists.

Father Collins, however, was placed in an almost impossible position by attorney Jack Ridley, litigating for the defense. Sitting as a witness for the State against a woman who faces the death sentence if found guilty, he condemned execution as an unspeakable action. At the same time, he was forced to admit that he, as a priest, sees the abortion act as murder.

10

ABIGAIL SUFFERED for Bill. After the first few days, after the initial shock of being accused of murder, Abigail made her peace with events. She knew the South, she was of the South, she knew all the faces of the South. Bill was the stranger here, his horror unabated, a gentle, sweet, and reasonable man, slow in movement and as honest as a man could be. How many times at parties, seeing her vivacity, her delight at being among people she knew, and her spirits high with a couple of drinks, men had contrasted her behavior with the stolidity of her husband and had come on to her. She was hardly beautiful, but she had a delightful smile, a good solid body, and a manner of being aware of herself that drew men to her. The few times she had allowed men to fondle her or kiss her, she was filled with guilt and overly solicitous to Bill; but no matter how increasingly considerate of his needs she became in her guilt, she was certain not a breath of suspicion ever crossed his mind.

Here he was in a state of misery that she had to confront and attempt to alleviate. Again and again Bill had given way to Ridley when it came to the litigation process. It was Bill who had laid out the line of attack in the questioning of Bishop Collins, but he would not have dared to litigate it himself. It had been a delicate matter. As a Jew in the United States, you don't attack a Catholic prelate, you don't challenge his religious beliefs. When Jack Ridley suggested that Bill might take over the examination, Bill had pulled away. "No, no, no—it's nothing that a Jew should do, certainly not here."

Then how was he defending her? Abigail knew that it was tearing Bill to pieces; and now, with Rabbi Herschel Cohen as the next witness, Bill shied away again. "We have Haberman with us now," he argued. "He's one of the best criminal litigators in New York. He's Jewish, so he can open up against the rabbi without fear of being charged with anti-Semitism. Don't you think I'd give anything in the world to do what Jack did—handling a Roman Catholic with kid gloves and yet getting what he had to get?"

"Because you gave it to him," Abigail insisted. "You laid out the line of attack."

"No. Because he's the South and because he's a Baptist, and because with all this going on, he and Button take themselves to church every Sunday morning. The only time I ever set foot in a church or a synagogue is to give a speech or take part in a panel discussion. Don't make it worse, Abby. I let you down. I know that."

"You never let me down," she said with annoyance.

"I'm not Jack Ridley."

"You're more than Jack Ridley could ever be. Can't you understand that?"

"Come on, Abby, I'm no part of this, I don't belong here. I know what you want, and damn it, I'm a lawyer, and you want to feel that I have enough guts to stand up to these bastards and fight them. That would be good for my ego, but Jack is one of them, and he's a better litigator than I could ever be."

"No. He isn't. You have something else—" She believed that—or did she? This man she had married was like a rock. He'd always be there. But she had never known him to be frightened before. He was frightened now, frightened at the thought of what might happen to her, frightened of the town, the rednecks, the hatred that simmered in the hot sun like a miasma. And she was frightened, too, for herself, and for Bill.

When Jack Ridley finished questioning the bishop, Abigail tried to bring herself to congratulate him in front of Bill, but she couldn't. She had not felt this way since the children were small, when she knew that without question she would lay down her life for them if need be. Now Bill was her child; she felt all rigid and defensive, not of herself or her case, but of Bill, as if to heal his pain were more important than any part of the trial.

Watching her, Button asked, "Are you all right, Abigail? Don't fret. Bill will survive."

"But will my marriage survive?"

"Sooner than mine will, love," Button assured her. "He'd never leave you. He adores you."

"And he feels that as a lawyer and defender, he's been a washout. Damn it, today Jack was brilliant."

"Brilliant is easy for Jack. Common sense, love, understanding—those come harder."

Haberman too felt that Jack had been damn clever, if not brilliant. "You took just the right tack, not too heavy, not too light. The jury will remember the bit about the scientist."

"I was an actor given a part," Jack said. "Bill here laid it out, every bit of it."

"Of course. That's proper teamwork. The words are the base, but a good litigator should be an inspired actor." He reached out to squeeze Bill's arm. "I read your notes for the rabbi. I'll watch with great interest."

"I want you to do it," Bill said.

"Why?"

"Because I'm a lousy litigator, and I watched you once in a courtroom in New York."

"But you're her husband," Haberman argued. "You'll bring something to it that I couldn't possibly. Never."

"I can't do it. I can't risk Abigail's life, not with you here and available."

"I want you to do it, Bill," Abigail said quietly.

"I can't. Carl here is better."

Abigail did not for a moment believe that in this case Carl was better. It was something else, complex, frustrating. Before she married Bill, she had brought him home to meet her mother. The meeting went well. He was charming and gentle, winning over her mother completely. He had just finished law school, graduating with honors, and Abigail could see how relieved her mother was. Now, after all the years gone by, Abigail waited to see who her children, Hope or Leon, brought home to meet her and to meet Bill. But then, after that first meeting, at lunch with her mother, she asked, "Well, how do you like him?"

"I like him. I don't think he put on a face for me. He seems to be outgoing and natural, and he never once remarked on my southern accent. That puts him in the plus column. He's good-looking, and he's tall and well built. You're five feet nine—"

"Five eight and a half."

"Still, that limits the field. And he's very bright, isn't he? Is he a Catholic? Not that I mind, I have no—absolutely no religious prejudice."

"He's Jewish," Abigail said.

"Oh?"

"Does that make a difference?"

"What do you think?"

"I don't know why I should even think about it. I didn't know it until our third date, when he asked me to marry him."

"It never occurred to you that Goodman might be a Jewish name?"

"I guess not. But it did occur to you, Mother. Why didn't you mention it?"

Her mother shrugged.

And now, here in the airless room in the courthouse, where she tried to take at least a bite or two of one of the tasteless sandwiches Jim Cooper had provided, she was torn between her desire for Haberman to take on the cross-examination and use all his skill and experience in her defense and her desperate need to offer herself to Bill as the woman he must love and protect. It was a hodgepodge of the sorry cult of macho with its benighted fingers of male dominance reaching everywhere, in her mind as well as in this incredible trial.

It will be a long time, she told herself, before they straighten out this lunacy and horror of man versus woman. Even love doesn't do it.

"Bill," Haberman said gently, "if you really want me to, I'll take on the rabbi. But I can't do it the way you laid it out."

"Change it if you think it best. But why?"

"You're too far removed," Haberman said. "I'm told your family came here from Germany in the 1840s. Too many generations from Orthodoxy. Herschel Cohen's father came here from Poland in 1923. My father came here in 1914. My family were Orthodox Jews."

"I understand," Bill said.

"Except the part about China. I like that, and I'd like to use it." Haberman paused, aware of the tensions and emotional pools into which he had stepped. "Rabbi Cohen," he said, "has his congregation in Brooklyn, poor, hardworking people for the most part. He's no fool, and he's filled with belief—just as the bishop was. I mention this simply to explain my departing from your projection."

"There is no need to explain," Bill said. "I'm not hurt, my feelings aren't injured. My God, if this is going to help Abigail, that's all that matters."

July 19. Moshe Katz, special to *Ha Shem,* Tel Aviv:

Today, Rabbi Herschel Cohen takes the stand, witness for the State; and this is not the least of the surprising convolutions this trial has taken. While some of my American colleagues, whose antennae are less sensitive than mine, will deny the presence of more than usual anti-Semitism here in Clarkton, I seem to feel it quite strongly. Perhaps for that very reason, they have imported Rabbi Cohen from Brooklyn, New York, a fallback if they are charged with undue anti-Jewish prejudice.

On the other hand, I find this prejudice here in the South difficult to understand. Jews have been here since the eighteenth century, and their enlistment in the Confederate forces during the American Civil War was higher, percentagewise, than among their Christian brethren. Yet the prejudice exists, eagerly embraced when something like this Abigail Goodman trial takes place.

Eileen Mott, covering the trial for the *New York Globe,* says it is a class thing, a redneck—a local term for the white underclass—spin-off of their fear and hatred of the blacks. She holds that since the gains made in the 1960s and 1970s, the struggle and competition for low-paying jobs has increased this bitterness; and historically it has always been easy to turn such hatred against the Jews.

All the more amazing to discover Rabbi Cohen here testifying for the prosecution. According to my New York colleagues, Rabbi Cohen has a local reputation in Brooklyn of being a liberal of sorts, pressing for joint effort by poor Jews and poor blacks to force the city to provide better housing and better education.

Nevertheless, he is totally dedicated to the Right to Life movement, as the anti-abortionists are called. Religion makes strange bedfellows indeed.

11

LIKE BISHOP COLLINS, Rabbi Cohen was tall, lean, and dark-eyed. His white beard and mustache were luxuriant, and the deep frown lines over his nose suggested the moral rigidity of a Savonarola, rather than the compassionate image to be expected of a rabbi. His thin lips were set firmly, and he regarded the courtroom, audience, judge, and jury with cold curiosity; and since so many there had never before seen a rabbi in the flesh, the curiosity was returned.

Haberman studied him with interest, anticipating what would occur when the clerk offered the Bible for the rabbi to take the oath. Instead of placing his hand on the Bible, the rabbi took it from the clerk, opened it, took his reading glasses out of the black suit he wore, and flipped through the pages of the Bible. Taken aback, the clerk did not interfere, and when the rabbi handed the book back to him, he received it obediently without protest.

At the defense table, Haberman whispered, "Oh, this is something indeed."

"What is it?" Abigail asked him.

"I don't think he'll take the oath."

"Rabbi Cohen," the judge said, "would you please take the oath."

His voice without an accent, clear, hard, and resonant, Rabbi Cohen said, "I will not."

"What do you mean?"

"In the first place, what you offered me is not the Holy Bible. It is the Word of God plus the New Testament."

Benson hesitated. This was new ground for him. He thought about it for a long moment, and then he said, "In this court, Rabbi, this book is regarded as the Holy Bible."

"Yes," the rabbi agreed, "in this court, but not in my mind or heart. In any case, I will not swear an oath, which in my faith is forbidden to me."

The judge stared at the rabbi, then pointed to the attorneys. "Would you approach the bench?"

When they stood in front of him, he said, "Any suggestions, Mr. Anderson? He's your witness."

"He agreed to testify. If you think it was easy getting a rabbi to testify—"

"Charley, don't be a horse's ass. Did he agree to take the oath?" The judge's whisper came out a hiss of anger.

"I never thought to ask him."

"Mr. Haberman, do you have any suggestions?"

"Why don't you ask the rabbi, Your Honor."

The attorneys went back to their places. The courtroom was already thick with whispers, and Benson banged his gavel for silence, then said to Rabbi Cohen, "I don't have to tell you, Rabbi Cohen, that you place the court in a predicament. Ordinarily, a witness who refused to take the oath would be found in contempt. I don't want to find you in contempt. Have you any suggestions?"

The rabbi reached into his jacket pocket and brought out a black book, about three-quarters of an inch thick, and handed it to the judge.

The judge opened it.

"You will not make much of it, unless you read Hebrew. It is what we call the Torah, the first five books of the Holy Bible, namely, Genesis, Exodus, Leviticus, Numbers, and Deuteronomy, set down by Moses as the Word of God. Now, if you wish me to hold this holy book in my hand while I state that I will speak the truth, I can do so. But I will not swear or take an oath."

The judge looked at Anderson. "Well, Charley?"

"I can accept that."

"And Mr. Haberman?"

"There's no difference to my way of thinking."

Anderson consulted his notes. He was on uncertain ground as he asked for identification.

"Rabbi Herschel Moses Cohen."

"You are a practicing rabbi?"

"If you call it so, yes."

"Meaning that you officiate not only in prayers, but in circumcisions"—he took a moment to glance at his notes again—"Bar Mitzvahs, marriages, and deaths?"

The rabbi permitted himself a trace of a smile, causing Abigail to remark to Button how restrained both these clergymen, Catholic and Jewish, were when it came to humor.

"A danger to the profession," Button whispered caustically.

"And your congregation is in Brooklyn, New York?"

"That's right."

"Is it a large congregation?"

"We have five hundred and twenty-two families."

"Very substantial," Anderson said. "Very substantial indeed. Now tell me, Rabbi, what is the attitude of your religion toward abortion?"

"It is forbidden—unless it is necessary to save the life of the mother. Otherwise, it is regarded as the murder of the child."

Anderson turned to the jury and, speaking to the rabbi, said, "Regarded as the murder of the child. Am I correct in repeating what you have said?"

"Yes. But that does not mean that I approve—"

"That's all, please. You have answered my question." And turning to Haberman, "Your witness, Mr. Haberman."

Seated at the defense table, Haberman muttered, "I don't believe it, I just can't believe it. Can he be that stupid, Ridley?

He doesn't learn. He never even tried to connect him with the accusation."

"He works at it. They don't need brains. First the verdict, then the trial."

"Are you ready, Mr. Haberman?" the judge asked.

"In a moment, Your Honor," and then to Jack, "Watch. This is not *Alice in Wonderland*." Haberman pushed back his chair and took a position at the end of the jury box.

"Rabbi Cohen," he said, "after you answered the last question the district attorney put to you, it appeared to me that you were trying to say that you did not approve of the charges brought against Mrs. Goodman. Is that so?"

On his feet, Anderson's objection held that Haberman was not only leading the witness, but putting words in his mouth.

"You opened the door," Benson said. "You didn't ask for his words to be stricken. They are in the record. Mr. Haberman has every right to ask what the words meant."

"Would you please answer my question, Rabbi Cohen."

"I believe abortion to be an undefendable sin against God, but death? No."

"But if abortion is the taking of a human life, why not the death penalty?"

"It is too cruel."

"Thank you. Then you believe Ms. Goodman to be guilty of a grievous sin, but not so grievous that she should pay for it with her life? Is that so?"

"I am not excusing her. I said it is too cruel."

"Ah, so you did. Now tell me, Rabbi, what is a sin?"

"Disobedience to God's commandment." He held up his hand to show that he had not finished his definition. "Going against the will of God."

"And how do we know what is the will of God? I ask you this because most of the people in this courtroom are Christians. Jewish theology is little known to them."

"I'm sure they know what is the will of God. The will of God, the commandments of God, the teachings of God—all of this exists in the holy book we call the Bible, what is known in English as the Old Testament. All of it is holy and inspired by God, but the Torah, the five books of Moses, taken down by him as he listened to the voice of God, these are the holiest."

"And, of course, as a learned rabbi, you know the books of the Bible."

"I do."

"And I am certain that when it comes to Exodus and Leviticus and the others of the first five books, you can quote pages by heart."

"I could. But in Hebrew, not in English."

"All the better, for with your knowledge of the original Hebrew, there would be less chance of an error in interpretation. You agree, don't you, Rabbi?"

"Of course."

"Very good. Now, Rabbi, would you please tell me where in the Holy Bible there is any proscription of abortion?"

"The Bible? I don't know what your understanding of the Bible is."

"Then let me spell it as you just did: according to Orthodox

Jewish belief, the five books of Moses, the first five books, which
you specified a moment ago, are called the Pentateuch, or in
Hebrew the Torah. These are the first five of the sacred canon-
ical books, as you well know, but I must underline them for the
record. These are also the most sacred books—"

"All of the Bible is sacred," Rabbi Cohen interrupted.

"Of course. Now the whole of the Bible is divided into three
parts. I speak of the Old Testament, Torah, Neviim, and Ketu-
vim." He paused to spell out the words for the stenographer.

"These are Hebrew words," Haberman continued.

"Mr. Haberman," the judge said, "can you get on with it. If
this is part of a question, make your question. I don't know why
we require liturgical lectures."

"Because without some explanation, the question would be
confusing to the jury and perhaps to the bench, Your Honor."

"Suppose you let me decide what my level of confusion is.
Now get on with it."

Watching Anderson, Abigail saw him half rise, as if to object,
and then drop back onto his chair each time.

"He's confused," Button whispered. "He doesn't know which
side is up. He's never been into anything like this before."

"Forgive me, Your Honor," Haberman said, and then to the
rabbi: "I translate those three Hebrew words thus: Pentateuch,
Prophets, and Hagiographa. Is that an acceptable translation?"

"Yes."

"And they comprise the twenty-four sacred books? Is that not
so?"

"Yes."

Haberman walked to the defense table and picked up his notes. "Rabbi Cohen, I will read the names of the books of the Holy Scripture and ask you to agree that they constitute the Old Testament, the Bible as Jews recognize it—"

"Mr. Haberman," Benson interrupted, "I think almost everyone in this court is familiar with the names of the books of the Old Testament. I am sure Mr. Anderson will stipulate to that. Can we go on?"

Anderson nodded.

"Very well. Now tell me, Rabbi Cohen, is there anywhere in those twenty-four books any paragraph, statement, phrase, if you like, commandment, dictum, any words that can be taken as a proscription of abortion? I asked you this question in a general sense. Now I ask it very specifically, very seriously. I demand an equally serious answer."

"It is commanded that one must not spill his seed vainly—"

"No, Rabbi, I am not talking about masturbation or coitus interruptus. I asked the question about abortion."

"As I see the reference in the Torah, it applies not to masturbation, but to birth control."

"We are not talking about birth control. We are talking about abortion. You stated that you know the Bible, that you accept it in part as the very word of God, in part as inspired by God. You stated that you had read the Holy Scripture so often that you knew whole sections by heart. If your memory fails, I will give you an Old Testament and the whole night to study it—"

"That's insulting!"

169

"No more insulting than the threat that faces my client. I ask you again—where is the reference to abortion?"

The rabbi sighed and shook his head. "There is none."

"There is none. Then how can you sit there, professing to tell the truth, and tell this court that God regards abortion as unforgivable and as murder?"

"Because it is part of my holy teachings and guides, the Talmud regards abortion as unforgivable."

"You speak of the Talmud. The Talmud is not the Bible, is it? I ask this to avoid confusion."

"No, it is not."

"What is the Talmud?"

"It is the oral law of the Jews, so-called because it existed in part before it was recorded. It consists of the teaching of the sages." The rabbi hesitated, thought about this for a long moment, and then said, "The teaching of the sages is inspired by God."

"Yes, we could say that all great works of literature are inspired by some holy spirit, but we are talking about another matter entirely. You do not put the Talmud in the same category as the Bible. You testified that the Bible is the Word of God. Is the Talmud the Word of God?"

"No, it is not."

"Thank you, Rabbi. And since there is no mention of abortion in the Bible, we have absolutely no divine decree on this question?"

"Jewish law," Rabbi Cohen replied, angry now, "is not a matter of what is written, but what the sages decree the written word to mean!"

"Would you answer yes or no, please. I ask you whether there is any divine guidance in the Bible on abortion?"

"When you put the question that way, I must answer no."

"Ralph Contain, the sinologist, has stated that if China outlawed abortion for five years, a million people would die of malnutrition and starvation. Would you still, in the face of such facts, outlaw all abortion?"

"I cannot comment on the situation in China. I don't know what the situation in China is."

Anderson was already on his feet, crying out that this all called for a conclusion.

"I'll sustain the objection, Mr. Anderson. And where are you going, sir?" he asked Haberman. "You're off the mark."

"I'm sorry, Your Honor."

"Are you through with this witness?"

"Just another question or two." Haberman paused to let the jury see that he was unhappy to have to confront the rabbi.

"Have you heard, Rabbi, of Joshua Keppleman?"

"Of course."

"Will you tell the jury who he is?"

"An Orthodox rabbi."

"A very important and revered Orthodox rabbi—is that not so?"

"If you feel that way. I don't."

"Now I quote from an interview with Rabbi Keppleman in *The Washington Post* of this past November." Haberman took a press clipping out of his pocket.

Anderson rose to object that the press clipping had not been entered as evidence.

"Mr. Anderson," the judge said patiently, "he is not introducing evidence; he is simply refreshing his memory. There is a difference. If he hands the clipping to the bench and asks that it be entered as evidence, it then becomes evidence. Do you understand? Now, Mr. Haberman, do you wish that to be entered as evidence?"

"No, Your Honor. I am simply refreshing my memory."

"Yes." And to Anderson, "You are overruled, sir."

"In answer to a question, Rabbi Keppleman states, 'An embryo is not a human being. It has no memory, no soul, no conscience, no contract with the Almighty as to behavior. It takes its place among mankind or womankind at the moment of birth.' End quote. Rabbi Cohen, do you know of this position taken by Rabbi Keppleman?"

"I do."

"And is he an Orthodox Jew?"

"So he calls himself. He is not a Hasid."

"But he is an Orthodox rabbi in the Jewish faith?"

"Yes."

"Very well," Haberman said, gentle now. "Only a few more questions. You see, in all my previous questions we discussed your competence in the field of religion. But Professor Goodman is not being charged with religious backsliding, but with what this state has declared a capital crime—abortion. Now, Rabbi, were you privy to any such abortion?"

"I was not."

"Then how do you know about this alleged crime of Mrs. Goodman's?"

"I was informed by Mr. Anderson and shown the indictment."

"Only that? You have no other evidence of the alleged crime?"

"No. None."

"Thank you. I have no other questions."

July 20. Freda Hammond, special to *The Times* of London:

There is a dark side to American society that one is highly conscious of here in Clarkton, USA, and last night's events have done nothing to lighten it. Yesterday, I sat in the courtroom where Abigail Goodman is on trial for her life, and I watched Carl Haberman, the distinguished New York lawyer who offered his services pro bono, engage in a masterly piece of cross-examination.

After court, Haberman dined with Abigail Goodman, William Goodman, Jack Ridley, the local lawyer who heads the defense team, and Button Ridley, his wife and partner. After dinner, at about half-past nine, Carl Haberman took his leave and drove home in a rented car. With all of his influence on the national scene, Mr. Haberman had been unable to find accommodations in a local hotel or inn, and he had made arrangements to stay with a relative, Joseph Klein by name, a shopkeeper in Clarkton.

Mr. Haberman had informed the Kleins that he would have dinner in town and would return to their house afterward, but no later than eleven o'clock. He was driving a rented Ford, a small car. When Mr. Haberman did not arrive at the Kleins' home by midnight, they became alarmed and telephoned William Goodman at his hotel. Goodman told Mr. Klein that Carl Haberman had parted with his dinner companions shortly after ten o'clock, and that it should have taken no more than fifteen minutes for him to drive back to the Kleins' place.

Convinced that Mr. Haberman had been in harm's way, Mr. Goodman called Jack Ridley, chief counsel in the legal team defending Abigail Goodman. The two men then went to the police station and convinced the local policeman in charge to send out what they call in the States an all points bulletin.

Nothing more was discovered that night, but early this morning Mr. Haberman's car was located in a creek (a large brook in local usage), at a place called Mill Hollow. A bridge goes over the creek at that point, and Mr. Haberman's car had gone through a guardrail into the creek below. The car was partly submerged. Left for dead, Mr. Haberman managed to make his way out of the car onto the bank, where he was found at dawn, badly injured but still alive. He had been savagely beaten, incurring a broken leg, a skull fracture, and some internal injuries. Fortunately the local hospital boasts a competent trauma team, and when I spoke to the physician in charge, I was told that while Mr. Haberman's condition was critical, they had every expectation that he would pull through without any permanent damage.

Being a woman gives me certain natural advantages, and it is amazing that even here in this dreadful, backwater place, an English accent appears to fascinate people. I had struck up an acquaintance with Jim Horst, the local police chief—at the hotel bar, I may say—and this has proven useful. Chief Horst claimed that he was surprised by the attack and the viciousness of it. In years past, such beatings were more common, perpetrated against blacks. He claims he has not seen a beating as vicious as this where a white man was the victim.

I can bear testimony to that. I am no stranger to violence. I covered the Gulf war, and I have done stories on the violence in Belfast, but I have never encountered anything like this.

"What kind of people would do something like this?" I asked Police Chief Horst.

"These are not people," he replied. "I mean the way you folks over there in England would think about people. I guess there is no way you can explain it to a Brit. They're the lowest white trash we have, and it ain't only that they hate Jews, they hate everybody. But if you're asking me, Miss Hammond, what they hate most is women, and this county has got more rapes per hundred of the population than any county in the state. Mr. Haberman comes down here, and even myself with an open mind, I got to feel it's some smart-alecky Jew from New York— believe me, I'm not anti-Semitic, but it's the way I feel—and he's going to put us all in our place. You understand me?"

It was not easy or nice, but I understood him.

"So these rednecks and river trash, they grab this little guy, and everything they hate goes into it."

"Do you know who did it?" I asked the chief.

"Maybe yes, maybe no. I got a lot of ideas, and I'll be pulling creeps in all day long. But nobody's going to admit to anything."

On the other hand, to Professor Goodman and her husband, this was a totally devastating event. Not only had Carl Haberman joined their defense, he had promised to place half a dozen of the younger members of his firm at the disposal of the defense. These things are done differently here than in England, and very important trials, where the money involved might run into millions simply as legal fees, tend to involve a small army of attorneys. The Goodmans have very little money, but Haberman was willing to place all the resources of his firm at their disposal pro bono. Now that opportunity has disappeared.

I have not been able to talk to the Goodmans or to the Ridleys since news of the attack on Mr. Haberman, but I did manage a short interview with Jim Cooper, a young law student who is part of the defense team. Our discussion follows:

"You can't imagine how badly this hits us," Cooper told me. "Haberman brought us a real ray of hope. Now the ball is back in our court. Oh, we'll fight it through all right, but we lost something. That makes it hard."

"Have you heard from his law firm? That would be his partners, wouldn't it? Most American law firms are partnerships, aren't they?"

"Yes, they are. Yes, Mr. Ridley spoke to Haberman's partners just a couple of hours ago. They were understandably upset."

"Will Haberman's firm continue with the case?"

"They're not ready to answer that yet, but the impression Mr. Ridley got is that they will not continue with the case. It seems that Mr. Haberman's partners were against Mr. Haberman's involvement, and this has only served to firm up their position."

"Do you know how Professor Goodman is responding to all this?"

"She's terribly upset. Mr. Ridley told the judge that under these circumstances, the trial cannot go on."

"Did the judge agree with him?"

"No, not at all. He gave us this day, and he wants us to be in court tomorrow."

"Will Mr. Ridley call for a mistrial?"

"I'm not sure. If he does, I don't think that the judge will grant one."

"What do you think of the judge's behavior?"

"I can't comment on that. It would be very improper of me."

"You know, Mr. Cooper, I write for a British audience. I suspect the feeling in Britain about violence in America is such that they will regard what happened here as normal. Do you agree with that?"

"As a black man who grew up here in the South, I might be tempted to say what happened here yesterday was normal, but no—that would not spell out the situation here. Mind you, I give you only my own opinion, but it seems to me that what is exploding here is a backlash against every gain women have

made since the 1960s. The trial of Professor Goodman symbol-
izes that backlash on the governmental level. The attack on Carl
Haberman is the same thing operating on the lowest level—the
kind of demented hatred of women that leads to rape and wife
battering. Well, that's my opinion, whatever it's worth. Talk to
someone else, like my boss, Mr. Ridley. He'll tell you it's the Ku
Klux Klan. That's just a name for scum. Doesn't change what I
said, no matter what you call it."

According to Jim Horst, the local police chief, "There are
rednecks over in the swamp country who will kill anyone they
take a dislike to for fifty cents, and it don't matter a damn bit
whether it's a Jew lawyer from New York or a classy Brit like
yourself. They just don't give a damn."

12

COURT CONVENED at ten o'clock. After the courtroom filled and the jury had taken their places, the clerk informed the lawyers that the judge would see them in chambers.

Bill and the Ridleys marched into the judge's chambers, along with Charles Anderson and Mike Sutter, his assistant, leaving behind them a buzz of curiosity and anticipation. By now everyone in the court knew that Haberman had been severely beaten and hospitalized.

In his chambers, Judge Benson said, "I am sure you know what I am going to say. They found Carl Haberman. He had gone off the bridge at Mill Hollow, and he was in the car. Since

Mill Hollow is ten miles out of town, we must accept the fact that he was deliberately attacked. Whether the attack has a direct connection with this case is not yet certain. It's a conclusion one could make, but until we find the culprits, it's only a surmise."

"Now, Charley"—turning to Anderson—"have you anything to add to this?"

"I'm afraid not. I consider it an outrage."

"We all do, Charley." And turning to Ridley, "Jack?"

"We will move for a mistrial."

"No," Benson said. "I am not going to grant a mistrial. Mr. Haberman joined your defense only the day before yesterday."

"That doesn't make him less vital," Bill argued.

"I want to make myself absolutely clear on this question. I will not grant a mistrial. You may ask for a continuance, and I will grant it only to the extent of twenty-four hours. But not a mistrial."

"Still, we must ask for it and put it on the record."

"If you must."

Going back into court and to the defense table, Bill Goodman asked Jack Ridley, "What the devil goes on here?"

"I don't know."

"Does he think someone attacked Haberman because Haberman's an outsider, that it has nothing to do with this trial?"

"Benson's a curious man, and he isn't stupid. He knows why Haberman was beaten."

"Then why no mistrial? It calls for it. If he denies us that, he's in error and he must know that."

"Of course. Maybe he doesn't give a damn whether he's in

error or not. Maybe he's looking for reversal. Or maybe there isn't any reversal. Our state supreme court is a rubber stamp for the governor, and as for the Supreme Court in Washington— well, I don't have to draw any diagram about them. They don't have to grant certiorari. And they're the end of the line. Bill, I don't know—I'm losing hold. This is not the world or even the state or the town that I grew up in."

Back in her room, Abigail could not excise the flow of pictures: Haberman's car stopped, the little man dragged from his car, beaten into unconsciousness, his skull smashed, then stuffed back into the car and driven to Mill Hollow, and the car pushed over the old wooden bridge and into the creek below, not far certainly from where she once sat with her grandfather, fishing for catfish.

Bill's physical reaction was simple and direct. He sat at her room telephone for hours, until he tracked down both of the children in Europe, and then he said to each of them, flatly: "You are not to come here under any circumstances. You will go directly to school."

When they pleaded with him that they belonged at Abigail's side, he exploded with an anger they had never experienced before. "No," he told his son, "you will not come here and you will not join me, and you will do as I say and you will not argue with me!"

Abigail listened to the explosion of anger, and when it was done and when he had spoken to their son and daughter and elicited pledges that they would not return to the place where they were born and educated, or to Clarkton, she said to Bill gently, "We must live here. Hilden is two hundred miles from here, but it's the same state, and it's our home, and it's the place where I teach and where you practice law, and it's a place the kids love—"

"No more!" Sharp and clean.

"You don't mean that."

"Oh, I do, I do—and you are still living with illusions. I have no illusions left. I have taken a long course, and I am finally learning not only what it means to be a woman in America, but what it means to be a woman here in this state, where all the courtly deference of antebellum still persists, and where your sex is honored by southern gentlemen. No, thank you!"

She had no reply to that.

The following day, when Judge Benson took his seat, Jack rose and asked for a mistrial. The judge beckoned him and, when Ridley stood in front of him, said softly, "We have been through this, Jack. I think you're behaving like a goddamned fool."

"If that is your opinion, Your Honor."

The judge stared at him a long moment. Then he said, "Motion denied." As Jack continued to stand in front of him, Benson said, "Let's get on with it, Mr. Ridley." He paused, then, "Mr. Ridley, if you desire a further continuance, I am prepared to give you another week."

"Could I have a moment?"

The judge nodded, and Jack went to the defense table. "I think we ought to take a continuance," Jack said.

Abigail said, "No! Go ahead!"

182

"Abigail, you're wrong," Bill told her. "He will give us a week, and we need it and we should take it."

Button agreed with Abigail. "There's something going around in my mind—why no mistrial? You know, if he called a mistrial, they'd take him off the case. He hates Anderson. Abigail's right. Let's go for broke."

Jack asked to approach the bench. "We want the trial to continue," he said. "I'd like Mr. Anderson to call his next witness."

"As you wish," Judge Benson agreed.

"They have two witnesses left," Button whispered to Abigail.

"I know. Is Bill taking Burger?"

"He was going to, but then he gave it to Haberman."

"Why?"

"Because, damn it, he loves you," Button said. "Don't you understand that? He's not a litigator, and he knows damn well that he isn't. Do you think for a moment you could have lived the life you tell me you lived with Bill, if he were a litigator? Tell me about litigators. They're all supermen, egomaniacs, and the best are the worst. They're worse than surgeons or generals; they're actors who write their own scripts, and they live by the belief that they can talk anyone into anything. That's what makes them good—good liars, among other things. I'm married to one, so I know what I'm talking about. We stay married because I'm as good a litigator as he is. We fight like cats, but it's an even match."

Abigail listened in amazement. She felt foolish. She had always believed herself to be sophisticated, learned, wise.

"And believe me, if we hadn't been in this night and day with Bill never out of your sight, my dear husband would have been in your pants. Oh, the hell with that. I love him. He's as horny as an old rooster, but he's good and he's decent."

"But who's taking the witness?"

"I am," Button said.

Anderson was already into his examination of Dr. Burger as his next friendly witness. Burger, stout, solid, blue eyes behind his glasses, thinning blond hair, was almost the ideal TV commercial stand-in. He was fifty-nine years old, chief of obstetrics at Grace Hospital in Brooklyn, New York, a Lutheran, and a deacon at his church. He had five children.

All of this Anderson rapidly extracted from him, and then he asked his proper lead-in question:

"What is your feeling about abortion, Dr. Burger?"

"Abortion is murder," he said flatly.

"All abortion?"

"All abortion," Burger replied. "Suppose you had a mature paraplegic, brain-damaged and retarded? Does that give you the right to murder him? That is my position on abortion."

"Anderson couldn't have thought of that one in a hundred years," Ridley whispered.

"And tell me, doctor, at what point do you consider the embryo to be a human being? The first trimester, the second trimester, or the third trimester?"

"I cannot approach it that way. At the moment of conception, we have, potentially, a human being. So there is only a technical difference between an abortion after the first two weeks of pregnancy or an abortion after the second trimester. In both cases, we are dealing with what is potentially a human being."

"I see." Anderson savored this for a long moment. "And there are no exceptions to your way of thinking?"

"None."

Anderson was taking no chances on opening doors that might lead to unknown territory. "Your witness," he said to the people at the defense table.

Button Ridley rose and came around the table to face Dr. Burger. She was five feet four inches tall, a head of straight brown hair turning gray, small nose, slate-colored eyes, and a quizzical smile on a full mouth. Abigail had never thought of her as a beautiful, or even as a very attractive woman, but at this moment, dressed so simply in a black linen skirt and a white blouse, she appeared to be very attractive indeed.

"Ms. Ridley." The judge nodded. "You'll be doing the cross-examination?"

"You have no objections, Your Honor?" Button asked, smiling.

"None."

"Thank you," Button said with just the slightest indication of a curtsy. Judge Benson had a heavy southern inflection in his speech. Button's speech matched it, although a few minutes before, talking to Abigail, she had had little southern accent, if any.

"That being the case," Judge Benson said, "and having started late, suppose we adjourn now until one o'clock. That will give us an hour and a half for lunch, and perhaps we can finish with this witness this afternoon."

Jack Ridley and Bill Goodman took the lunch break to go to

185

the hospital and see Haberman. During an earlier visit, the physician in charge, a Dr. Clement Lederer, told them that it was best to put off any conversation with Haberman, as he was heavily medicated and in no condition to talk. Now they were permitted to enter his room, where the little man lay, his eyes closed, his head swathed in bandages, his leg lifted and in a cast.

"He won't be able to speak very much," said the nurse on duty. "There appears to be a slight fracture in his jaw, and they haven't decided whether to wire it or not. His family asked that he be moved to New York, but Dr. Lederer advised against it—at least not for a while."

Haberman opened his eyes.

"You don't have to say anything," Bill said. "We're just sorry it had to happen. We're so damn sorry."

Haberman appeared to try to speak; then he closed his eyes.

"It's so painful for him to speak," the nurse said.

Chief Horst was downstairs, in the entryway of the hospital, and he asked Ridley, "What? Anything?"

"Nothing," Ridley said. "They busted his jaw. It probably hurts too much for him to say anything."

"Yeah. Well, I'll get a statement tomorrow or the next day."

"Who did it?" Ridley asked him.

Horst shrugged. "It's just too damn hot down here," he said, wiping his face with a wet handkerchief. "Air-conditioning's lousy. How many times I tell them this ain't no good for a hospital!" He was a heavy, red-faced man.

"Come on, Jim," Jack said.

"Let's get the hell out of here."

Back in the police station, Ridley put the question to him again.

"Jesus God, Jack, we only just started looking."

"There's no one in this town could pull off something like this except the Klan. You know that."

"Jack, the Klan's dead."

"Bullshit!"

"I told you we're working on it."

"So the Klan's enlisted with the Right to Life crowd," Ridley said. "That's beautiful. We walk out of here and there'll be a dozen reporters swarming around. We got reporters from countries you never heard of. What do I tell them? That there's a right to life for everyone but Haberman? That he's meat for murder because he isn't an embryo?"

"Tell them we are going to leave no stone unturned—absolutely no stone unturned—and we will find these bastards."

"That's beautiful. Write me a letter when you bring them in."

"Where you going to be?" Horst asked, grinning.

"Retired and maybe spending a summer in the Swiss Alps," Jack said tiredly.

"Now here's a Jew lawyer from New York driving around here in the middle of the night—what the hell, why didn't you tell him something?"

"Let's get out of here before I throw up," Bill said.

Abigail, meanwhile, had been delegated to talk by telephone to Carl Haberman's only child, a daughter, Clarissa Hendley. She was married to Gene Hendley, a New Jersey congressman, and when Abigail finally reached her, she had already heard the news. Sobbing, she listened to Abigail's account, and then she

187

put her husband on the phone. He asked Abigail a few questions about the situation at Clarkton and then told her that his wife would arrive in Clarkton late that afternoon, and could they make some arrangement for her accommodation. He had been told that not a hotel room remained unoccupied. He had already spoken to Dr. Lederer at the hospital and had talked Lederer into making arrangements to move Haberman by air ambulance the following day. He was cold as ice and let her know how ill advised he thought Haberman had been to enter the case at all. Tired, having had little sleep the night before, Abigail felt totally depleted. She tried to control her contempt for Gene Hendley—and for all the rest of the Congress he was a part of—but it was not easy. Meanwhile Rita Asbury and her sister, Essie, Jack Ridley's officer workers, were on the other lines, talking to Haberman's office, telling the mayor of New York City that they couldn't locate Mr. Goodman, putting the governor of New York on hold. Jim Cooper was trying to deal with the media, who had choked the entryway to the Ridley offices, and Button, after talking to Haberman's partner at the New York offices, was trying to drink from a container of coffee and write out her notes at the same time.

When Bill and Jack Ridley had fought their way back into the office with the aid of two policemen, Ridley said, "Button, you were wrong. Go in now and ask for a continuance."

"No. This is Anderson's last witness. The scuttlebutt is that he won't call his other witness. He's scared, and he has nothing. And as for that stinking pile of poor white trash that calls himself Dr. Steven Burger, I'll leave nothing of him."

"He's a New Yorker, and—"

"He'd be poor white trash if he came from Mars. Don't you see?" Button said. "They have nothing. They've proven nothing. They made no case, and that bastard Anderson isn't even trying. He knows how it ends, but does Benson? That's the question."

"What are you talking about?"

"You don't really know what's going on, not you, not Bill—not an inkling. You keep thinking we're fighting an abortion case. Look at it another way, damn it! It's the war against women—the war that's been going on for thousands of years. You think those people out there on the street, marching up and down in front of the courthouse, give two damns whether Abigail and I had an abortion or not? If they're so filled with love for life and the sanctity of life, why are they the first to cheer when we go to war? Why didn't they open up when we went to war in the Gulf and slaughtered a quarter of a million Arabs? They wrapped themselves in yellow ribbon and cheered it on. Why don't they protest for the thousands who die of AIDS every day? Why don't they talk about hunger and poverty? No way! It's the women—always the women."

"Button!" her husband exclaimed. "That is crazy talk. You're talking like a nut. You're all wet, and you're getting out of hand."

"I'm not getting hysterical, Jack. It's all right. I'm just letting out some of the steam I've bottled up these past weeks, while you guys talked and talked."

"Only that's no line for the jury."

"I'll do it my way. For God's sake, trust me."

When the court was convened at half-past one, Judge Benson called the attorneys to the bench and asked Anderson whether this was his last witness.

"I'm afraid so," Anderson admitted. "We asked two doctors and a nurse from Hilden Hospital as witnesses. They refused. The hospital manager refuses any cooperation whatsoever. We could subpoena any or all of them, but I don't think hostile medical witnesses are going to do us one bit of good. So we'll rest with this. I think we've made our case."

"And you're ready for Dr. Burger, Ms. Ridley?"

"I am indeed," Button said. She walked to the jury box, smiled at them, and nodded, as if they were old friends. Even the stony faces of some of the men relaxed under her smile. "I have a good memory," she said. "It doesn't mean I'm smart, but I'm a quick study, as actors say. It got me a lot of A's in school."

"Ms. Ridley?" the judge said.

"Yes, of course, Your Honor. I was simply explaining to the jury why I don't have to ask the stenographer to read back the record. Here is what Dr. Burger said: 'At the moment of conception, we have, potentially, a human being. So there is only a technical difference between an abortion after the first two weeks of pregnancy or an abortion after the second trimester. In both cases, we are dealing with what is potentially a human being.' " She turned to the doctor. "Have I quoted you correctly, Dr. Burger?"

"I think so."

She turned to the stenographer: "Have I quoted him correctly?"

"I think so."

"Would you read it, so that the jury may compare my quote to Dr. Burger's statement."

"Ms. Ridley," the judge said, "isn't that enough?"

"Well, Your Honor, I want it fixed in the minds of everyone in this courtroom. My husband, Mr. Ridley"—indicating Ridley to the jury—"thinks it's a clever trick and that the district attorney didn't invite it, but I think it's one of the stupidest statements I ever heard in all my life and right on the level of the district attorney—"

Anderson was on his feet, shouting an objection and demanding an apology from Ms. Ridley.

Benson banged with his gavel, trying to quell the laughter in the courtroom and threatening to have the court cleared. Then he said angrily, "Ms. Ridley, what are you up to? You know better, and let me say, if you are going to continue this cross-examination, don't try my patience. I think you owe an apology to Mr. Anderson."

"Your Honor, perhaps I do owe an apology to my husband and perhaps to Dr. Burger. I said his statement is stupid—not Mr. Anderson. I certainly do apologize to Mr. Anderson for anything I may have said that hurt his feelings."

"Is that sufficient, Mr. Anderson?"

"Yes, Your Honor."

"Then get on with it, Ms. Ridley, if we want to finish this afternoon."

"Would the stenographer read Dr. Burger's statement?"

"Again?"

"Please, Your Honor."

The judge sighed and spread his hands, and the stenographer read Burger's statement again.

"Thank you," Button said. "Now, Dr. Burger, I think your statement is well fixed in the minds of each and every person in this courtroom. You said that at the moment of conception, we have potentially a human being. Right?"

"Yes. I said that."

"Yes. Now, for a woman to become pregnant, a male sperm cell must unite with a female egg cell, and these together form, as you well know, a fertilized egg cell. Now again, a fraction of a second before the sperm met the egg, was the sperm potentially a human being?"

Taken somewhat aback, Dr. Burger stared at Button without answering.

"Take a moment to think about it," Button said, "and while you are thinking about it, tell me whether the egg cell of the woman was potentially a human being in that moment before they greeted each other?"

Benson pounded with his gavel as the room broke into laughter.

Dr. Burger came out of his mentation. "I cannot answer that question yes or no."

"But I am asking for an answer—yes or no. Do you refuse to answer the question?"

"It is theological. I am not a theologian."

"But you spoke with absolute assurance about the result of sperm and egg touching base with each other. That's the moment of conception, and at that moment, according to your testimony, a potential human being appears. According to Noah Webster, potential, when used as a noun, speaks of something that has the possibility of being actual. Will you deny that every sperm cell a human male produces in a lifetime has the potential of becoming a human being?"

Hesitating, "Would you repeat that question?"

"Certainly," Button said, crossing to the jury box, glancing at the jury with just a touch of her quizzical smile, as if she were letting them in on a secret spoof. "I ask you whether you would deny that every sperm cell a man produces in a lifetime has the potential of becoming a human being."

"I have to deny it, because these sperm cells have not encountered an egg cell."

"But how does that change the potential?" Button demanded. "If egg and sperm face each other a fraction of a second before fertilization, then each has the potential of producing a human being. I use your word. Potential, which means latency as well."

"Only together."

"But it is latent in each, is it not?"

"If you put it that way, yes. But until—"

"No, no!" Button snapped. "That's enough." She advanced on the doctor with such grim determination that he shrank back in the witness box. "And tell me, sir, have you ever masturbated? Have you ever had a wet dream? How many millions of your sperm cells have you consigned to destruction? No, no, don't answer me. The answer is evident in every man who walks on earth!"

Anderson was on his feet, shouting his objections. Judge Benson was pounding away with his gavel, and the court-room audience, media and public, were choking on their laughter.

"I will have order now!" Benson roared. "Or I will clear this court. And you, Ms. Ridley—you have overstepped all bounds!"

Button stood her ground, facing the bench.

Abigail watched her, enthralled with her, loving her, envying her. Jack spread his hands hopelessly, and Bill whispered excitedly, "Go for it."

Jim Cooper hissed, "That, folks, is an attorney."

"If she survives—if we both survive," her husband said.

And Button, firmly planted before the bench, said calmly, "No, Your Honor. I have not overstepped all bounds, with due respect, I have not. Mr. Anderson opened a door and I walked through it."

Benson stared at her, then shook his head and said, "Mr. Anderson, why are you on your feet?"

"I objected, Your Honor."

"To what? To her language?" He turned back to Button. "You have a witness on the stand, Ms. Ridley. Your reference to personal habits is both vulgar and out of order. Once more and I will put leniency aside." And to Anderson, "Sit down, please, Mr. Anderson. Your objection is overruled."

"Exception," Anderson said.

"I do not want to think of you as a mass murderer, no, no,

no," Button said to the doctor. "If anything I said gives that impression, I apologize to you."

Dr. Burger nodded. The judge watched her suspiciously.

"But, Dr. Burger," Button said, "that is because I do not believe in the potential human character of a lost sperm cell. Do you?"

Anderson rose to his feet, and Button said hastily, "I withdraw the question. Dr. Burger, you said your practice is in Brooklyn. Am I right?"

He muttered, "Yes."

"Speak up, please," Button said, smiling.

"Yes, my practice is in Brooklyn."

"In a poverty-stricken area, am I right?"

"Yes. I suppose so."

"What do you mean, you suppose so? You either know or you don't know. Your hospital receives a large sum of money each year from New York City to support a very large outpatient clinic. So I ask you again, are you in a poverty-stricken area? Yes or no?"

"Yes."

"Thank you. Doctor, tell me about an eleven-year-old child who carries a child to term? What is the usual fate of her baby?"

"Nonsense! Eleven-year-old children do not give birth to babies."

"Oh?" Button walked over to the defense table. Abigail handed her a notebook, and, studying the notebook, she returned to face Dr. Burger. "Dr. Burger, on November five of last year, Matilda Jones, age eleven, gave birth to a three-pound child. The child lived for three months. On December twenty-three, Hope Ginger, age eleven, gave birth to a five-pound child. The mother died of AIDS complications. On December twenty-seven, Angela Brown, age eleven, child stillborn. All at your hospital. Of the three, only one birth survived. What happened to that child and its eleven-year-old mother?"

"I don't know."

"You don't know," Button said with total contempt. "You don't know. You sit there as a witness in a trial of a good and loving woman for the crime of having an abortion at age forty-one, and you dare to tell me you don't know!"

"She is badgering the witness!" Anderson cried.

Judge Benson took no notice of Anderson's outcry, and Button consulted her notes again.

"Twelve years old. There's an excellent age for motherhood, wouldn't you say, Dr. Burger?"

"No, I would not."

"Last year, at your hospital, fourteen deliveries from children age twelve and thirteen. Did you know that, doctor?"

"Yes."

"Abortion is still legal in Brooklyn. Why weren't any of these births aborted?"

"The mothers were afraid to reveal their condition."

"By mothers you mean children, pregnant children aged twelve and thirteen. Am I right?" Button demanded.

"If you wish to call them children. Such is your privilege."

"My God, Dr. Burger, do I hear you right? You are a physician. You have taken the Hippocratic oath, and you dare to question whether an eleven-year-old or a twelve-year-old is a child?"

"She's at it again, Your Honor!" Anderson shouted.

"Just calm yourself, Mr. Anderson," the judge said, and, "Now, look here, Ms. Ridley, this is not a theater. You will please avoid personal reflections on the character of the witness."

"I will try, Your Honor."

"Yes. Please do."

"Now, doctor," Button said, "in the past twelve months, forty-three children were delivered at Grace Hospital whose mothers had AIDS. Do you know what is the fate of a child born of a mother who has AIDS?"

"Of course I do."

"Then would you please inform the jury."

"In almost fifty percent of the cases, the infant dies. It may survive a few years, sometimes five or six years, but if it has contracted AIDS from the mother, it dies."

"The infant dies—because its immune system is either damaged or totally destroyed. Is that so?"

"Yes."

"What causes the death of the infant?"

"Usually pneumonia or some other fatal disease. You see, the AIDS infant has no defense against disease."

"Then tell me, doctor, if a pregnant woman suffering from AIDS had an abortion, would that be murder?"

"Yes, it would."

"Better to let the child be born and then die perhaps weeks after birth?"

"According to my belief, yes."

"You have very strange beliefs, if I may say so, doctor. Were you paid to come here to Clarkton and be a witness in this case?"

"Yes, I was paid for my time. My time is valuable."

"How much were you paid?"

Anderson leaped to his feet with an objection. "He doesn't have to answer that question."

"It goes to the integrity of the witness!" Button cried.

"I'll let him answer it," the judge said. "We've had it out of other witnesses. You will answer the question," he instructed Burger.

"I was paid five thousand dollars."

"Lord-a-mercy, five thousand dollars," Button said, manufacturing a very real gasp. She turned to the jury. "Can you imagine, five thousand dollars just to sit for an hour in that chair. Goodness, that's better than the oldest profession."

On his feet again and pointing a finger, Anderson yelled, "That woman—that woman is turning this into a circus!"

"Ms. Ridley," the judge said after pounding with his gavel, "I have warned you again and again. Once more will be the end of my patience."

Button stood abashed, like a small girl caught with her hand in the cookie jar. "Is it not a circus?" she asked softly.

"Must I sit here and be insulted?" Burger wanted to know. "Do I have no rights?"

"I think your rights are adequately protected," Benson said. "Let's get on with this thing."

Button looked at her notebook again and then said, "According to Grace Hospital records, Medicare was charged over a hundred thousand dollars for surgery you performed. As for non-Medicare, well, what was your income last year?"

Anderson objected, and the judge said, "You will not answer that question, doctor. I want it stricken."

"It goes to the character of the witness," Button complained.

"We'll do without it."

"And is it true," Button said, "that you were reprimanded by the board of Grace Hospital because you refused to operate on AIDS patients?"

Anderson objected, and his objection was sustained.

Button stretched the silence before her next question. She returned the notebook to the table, fussed with the papers there, and then walked to the jury box. She sighed and turned back to the witness stand, then asked almost indifferently, "Dr. Burger, did you ever participate in an abortion?"

Silent, the doctor stared at her.

"Did you ever participate in an abortion?" Button asked again.

The courtroom became very silent, terribly silent. Dr. Burger licked his lips uneasily. Anderson, after a long moment, decided to come to his rescue and rose to his feet.

"I will not entertain an objection," the judge said, "so you might as well save your breath."

"The question has no pertinence," Anderson argued.

"It is completely pertinent," the judge said.

"Please answer my question," Button insisted.

"I don't know what you mean by participate," Burger said.

Button replied, "You have such difficulty with the language,

Dr. Burger—surely medical school requires a minimum of lit-
eracy. To participate in something means to take part in it or to
be a part of it. You are now participating in a trial. I am also
participating in a trial. A woman is on trial for premeditated
murder, accused of having an abortion. According to the law of
this state, anyone who participates in an abortion can be charged
with murder."

"It was thirty years ago. I was a student."

Anderson sprang to his feet, crying out that this should be
explained.

"Dr. Burger," Judge Benson said, "I think Mr. Anderson
wishes me to explain the nature of ex post facto, which simply
means that you cannot be prosecuted under a law that comes
into existence after the time of the alleged crime. In other
words, you cannot be held for an act committed thirty years
before the law in question was passed."

Dr. Burger appeared to rid himself of a fairly crushing burden. He breathed deeply and informed the court that he had
only been a student in a teaching hospital.

"You watch. You watch what happens in the hospital. It's a
part of teaching. All the medical students watch. Otherwise,
how could we—" He broke it off.

"What were you going to say, doctor? Please complete your
answer."

"I answered the question," Burger muttered.

"Were you going to say, how could we learn how to do an
abortion if we were not taught properly? Is that what you were
going to say?"

"She's leading the witness again," Anderson pleaded.

"I'll sustain that," the judge said. "You do know better, Ms. Ridley." This was mildly put. "You will ignore her statement," he told the jury.

Button walked to the defense table, riffled through some papers, whispered to her husband, "I don't hate all men. I still love you, I think," and then picked up a piece of yellow paper, stared at it thoughtfully, and then folded it.

"Would you get on with it, Ms. Ridley," the judge said.

"Oh, yes. Yes indeed." As she approached the witness, she glanced at the yellow paper again and then addressed the witness sharply. "Was that the only time you ever participated in an abortion, doctor?"

After a long moment, "Yes."

"You are certain?"

"Yes."

Button unfolded her sheet of paper once more. "It couldn't be a bit of a memory loss, could it, doctor? A convenient forgetfulness?"

"Absolutely not!"

"Dr. Burger," Button said, "I am going to give you a moment to search your memory, and I remind you that you are under oath and that the penalties for perjury are severe."

Anderson rose, but the judge waved him down. "Let's keep on with it, Mr. Anderson. If you are going to object each time Ms. Ridley ignores the boundaries of what you consider proper, we'll be here for a week."

"I ask you again," Button said to the witness. "Is the time you recall, the time when you were a student—was that the only time you ever participated in an abortion?"

"Well—well, perhaps—"

"Yes or no, please, doctor!"

"There was one other time—"

"One other time?" Button snorted. "One other time? Only one other time? And you come here as a witness for the prosecution? What else have you forgotten, doctor? My client, Ms. Goodman, is accused of having had an abortion. Have you any knowledge of such an abortion?"

"I have read the indictment."

"Oh? Bless your heart, you have read the indictment. Have you ever examined Ms. Goodman?"

"No, I have not."

"Then in true evidentiary terms, you have absolutely no knowledge of whether or not Ms. Goodman ever had an abortion. Is that not so?"

"No, it is not."

"Then please tell us what evidence you have."

"The district attorney's word," Burger said, regaining some measure of poise.

"And if the district attorney told you the world is flat, would you consider that as evidence?"

Anderson rose to his feet, but before he could speak, Benson waved a finger for him to be seated. "I'll allow it." Burger hesitated. "Answer her question," the judge said.

"That's different."

"So it is, so it is," Button agreed. "The fact is that you had absolutely no knowledge of whether Mrs. Goodman ever had an abortion. Is that not so?"

"I answered before—"

"Doctor, that's enough," Button said with disgust, and to Benson, "I have no more for this witness."

She strode back to the defense table, tossing the folded sheet of yellow paper onto the table. Abigail picked it up and looked at it. Nothing was written on it; the sheet was empty. Abigail refolded it to put it in her purse.

"No, give it to me, dear," Button said. She tore it into small pieces and dropped them into the wastebasket under the table.

"How did you know?" Abigail asked her.

"The doctor is a swine. There never was a medical swine who didn't do illegal abortions."

Meanwhile, Judge Benson, watching intently the disposal of the sheet of yellow paper, asked Anderson whether he had anything to add in redirect.

"No, Your Honor."

"Would you approach the bench?" Anderson went up to the bench, and the judge asked him softly, "Don't you want to give your witness an opportunity to deny these charges? They are charges by innuendo and without legal merit."

"I know that, sir," Anderson replied uneasily.

"Well, the ball is in your court, Mr. Anderson. You may go on now."

"As I said, I have no other witnesses."

"Yes, of course."

Anderson returned to his table, remained standing while the

judge dismissed the witness; then he said, "Your Honor, I have no other witnesses at this point. I believe that the State has presented its case, fairly and beyond any rational dispute—"

"Save the arguments for the closing, Mr. Anderson," the judge said. "It is enough to say that the State rests."

"Very well, Your Honor. The State rests."

"I am going to postpone the case for the defense until Monday," Benson said. "We will convene at ten o'clock sharp. Please be ready with your first witness, Mr. Ridley."

13

July 21. Frank Geller, special to the *Chicago Times:*

Today, District Attorney Charles Anderson examined his last witness and rested his case. To my way of thinking, Mr. Anderson has presented a close and unshakable case and has proved, at least to this correspondent's satisfaction, that Professor Abigail Goodman is guilty under the law. Rumor has it that the first witness for the defense will be Abigail Goodman, but it is not likely that the self-satisfied arrogance that marked all her statements to the press will endear her to this local jury of small-town folk, who think in simple and direct terms.

In all my questioning around town, I have yet to meet any

more than a handful of people who sympathize with Abigail Goodman. Her connection with Hilden College does not help. Hilden College, an Episcopal school in the northern part of the state, has long been known as a breeding ground for liberals. It was one of the first colleges in the South to have open admission for blacks, and today it has a 30 percent black student body, proportionally one of the largest in the South. In the 1960s, Hilden College faculty and students led the civil rights march on the state capital, and its antiwar demonstrations led the FBI to characterize it as a "Commie nest."

There have been, during the course of this trial, endless demonstrations in support of Professor Goodman. Practically all of the demonstrators have come from out of town, brought in by caravans of buses. The appearance of a dozen film stars did little to sway the opinions of the townspeople; and if the opinions of the townsfolk I have spoken to match the opinions of the jury, no defense that Mr. Jack Ridley, head of the defense team, may put on will increase the Goodman hope for a verdict of not guilty. During one of the press conferences held by the defense, Professor Goodman stated that she had done no wrong, broken no law, and had done nothing to apologize for. It is precisely this kind of arrogance that has put off so many observers.

The courtroom had been filled every day, but to Abigail, today, it appeared larger—more people, more faces, more threatening. It was too silent, strangely silent. Every other day, the court had been filled with chatter until Benson tapped with his gavel for silence.

"All rise!"

"Easy, love," Bill whispered to her. "Easy does it."

Benson watched the observers for a long moment, and Abigail asked herself, Who is he? What is he thinking?

Julia Hyde, of the City Press Syndicate, scribbled on her pad, "Abigail, beige linen skirt, beige linen jacket, brown shoes, off-white blouse, hair tied back—why can't she do her hair properly and make some points?—she could be so damned beautiful if she only tried, think what Vincent could do for her, she sits there with that enigmatic Giaconda half-smile, as if she were listening to her kids reporting on a day at school—"

"Mr. Ridley," Judge Benson said, "you reserved your rights on motions and introductory remarks. Do you have motions?"

Standing and crossing to half face the jury, Jack said, "Yes, Your Honor. I move to dismiss."

"Basis?" Benson asked.

"I have three points. First, the law as written provides cruel and unusual punishment. Second, by custom of most states in this country, criminal code number 157 is an ex post facto law, specifically in the *People* versus *Goodman*. And third, on the basis that the People have not proven their case."

"We have heard the first two parts of your motion before, and both are denied," Benson said slowly. "On the third part, the evidence presented by the prosecution does establish, according to my thinking, a prima facie case. The motion is denied. You may proceed to make your opening remarks."

"Yes, Your Honor," Jack Ridley said. "My colleague, William Goodman, will open, if the court please."

Benson nodded. "Proceed."

Bill had notes. He had been making notes since the trial began, and now all he could think about was a time fourteen years ago when he had been sure that Abigail had been unfaithful to him. He had volunteered as a baby-sitter, when they could find none. She had wanted desperately to attend a faculty dance, and on his part, he couldn't have cared less whether or not he was there, so he'd sat with the kids and then put them to bed, and then dozed off in front of a late movie on the TV, and then awakened at one in the morning, and then sat in misery until about two in the morning, and then crawled into bed, and at a bit past three he'd heard the car pull up and the car door slam. Three times during that night he had called the local police, and once he had called the hospital, and all of them said, No, there had been no accidents; so now he had turned over on his side and pretended to be asleep.

"I came in very late last night," she said in the morning.

"Oh? I was asleep."

"Wonderful," she said brightly. "When did you conk out?"

"I suppose around midnight," he answered indifferently.

"Thank goodness. Then you didn't worry?"

"Slept like a log."

Neither of them ever mentioned it again, and neither of them ever baby-sat for the other after that, and during the years that followed, he sometimes wondered about the fact that his suspicion mattered so little. He adored his wife. He never fully recovered from the shock of her willingness to marry him. His proposal was so tentative that it was almost withdrawn in the making, an inner voice asking how a stiff, awkward, bumbling character like himself even dared; and when she replied, "Of course I will. I thought you'd never ask," he simply stared at her openmouthed in disbelief.

And now he sat at the defense table with his pile of notes in front of him, remembering that time, annoyed at himself for recalling it, unable to think of any reason for recalling it now at this moment, thumbing through his notes, his mind suddenly empty.

Jack touched his shoulder. "Bill?"

He forgot the notes, rose, started toward the jury box, hesitated, thought of going back for his notes, shook his head and gave up on the notes, and then walked over and put his hands on the rail in front of the jury box. He was a big man, six feet and an inch, wide-shouldered, brown eyes, thinning gray hair, and an expression that seemed always to be questioning gently. He regarded the jurors thoughtfully for a long moment.

Then he said, "I'm William Goodman. Abigail, on trial here, is my wife."

He paused, entertained the thought of returning to the table for his notes, cast the thought aside, and looked from face to face. What is the face of a kind, thoughtful, bitter, or indifferent person? Criminals don't look like criminals; murderers don't look like murderers. Abigail had put her hope in a black woman who worked as a laundress, but now that women, Essie Lotus, looked at him with no kindness. Certainly she had her own agonies. He and Abigail were rich white folk. Why should she give a damn?

"It seems very strange," he went on, "that a woman as gentle and kind as my wife should be put on trial accused of the murder of a child she never had. I have been married to her for twenty-one years. I have never known her to perform an act of cruelty or unkindness—" He shook his head, his voice choking up. This was no way to make a plea. Where were all his years of experience as a lawyer? Why didn't he lay out the steps the prosecution had taken in the presentation of their evidence and demolish these steps, one by one? That was what any well-trained attorney would have done. And what now? he asked himself.

"You have listened to five witnesses for the People. Not one of them testified to anything that would even suggest that my wife is a criminal or has ever engaged in a criminal effort." He felt a little more confident. He had put together enough notes to speak for an hour, but, he realized suddenly, that was neither necessary nor profitable. Whatever he said, they would hear only what they wanted to hear.

"My wife," he said, his voice more firm, "is a fine and intelligent woman. We intend to prove that she is innocent of the charges brought against her. Whatever I might say of her character and behavior would be said out of the consuming love I have had for her since we first met and, of course, out of the consummate respect I have for her intelligence and understanding. She is to be the first witness for the defense, and her examination will be conducted by Ms. Ridley. It is the decision of our defense team that the litigation of our defense witnesses should be conducted by Button Ridley—since the charges presented in the courtroom are of such enormous consequences to women the world over. Let me say in conclusion that we had hoped to defend my wife with the aid of nationally known attorneys. However, the brutal attack on Carl Haberman put an end to that. Thus we come before you as small-town attorneys. We do not believe that these circumstances will affect your ability to hear the evidence, weigh it, and come to a fair and just decision."

Bill returned to the defense table and sat down next to his wife. Her hand reached out to his.

Judge Benson said, "Call your first witness, Ms. Ridley."

Abigail rose, walked to the witness stand, and took the oath. Button Ridley took her place at one end of the jury box as Abigail gave her name to the clerk.

"What was your maiden name, Professor Goodman?" Button asked her.

"Henderson. Actually, Abigail Lucy-Anne Henderson. I dropped the middle part. Up north they don't really understand the affection we have for middle names and hyphenated names. The Abigail comes from my grandmother, who was from Bennington in Vermont. Abigail is not a very common name here, but in New England—"

Anderson was on his feet objecting, and Benson said, "Softly, Mr. Anderson. She is simply answering Ms. Ridley's question."

"Your Honor, she is making a speech."

"No, Mr. Anderson, she is answering her counsel's question. Now would you both please approach the bench."

When Anderson and Button stood at the bench, Benson said quietly, "Mr. Anderson, the defendant is on the witness stand. As you know, she is not required to give testimony either for or against herself; therefore, it is only reasonable to give her a certain latitude. You have a propensity for objection, Mr. Anderson, and I do not intend to sit here for hours while you object to every small infraction that might exist in the laws of evidence. We want to look on the evidence, and then get this trial over with, the sooner the better. Do you understand me? I have given no preference to either side. I want this trial to be on the books. Now go on with your examination, Ms. Ridley."

"How old are you?" Button asked Abigail.

"Forty-one—well, truthfully, I'll be forty-two in September. That's only two months away. Perhaps it would be more honest to say forty-two."

"Yes, thank you," Button said. She was businesslike, direct, and plain. "How long have you been married?"

"Twenty-one years last month."

"And do you have children?"

"I have two children, yes."

"Would you tell us about them? Their names and ages."

"Leon is the elder—he is twenty. My daughter, Hope, is eighteen."

"Where are they now?"

"They are both abroad, traveling with student groups. They wanted desperately to join me here, but after the attack upon Carl Haberman, I forbade them—"

Anderson was on his feet. "I must object to this!"

Studying him coldly, Benson asked, "Why, sir?"

"The beating of Carl Haberman has nothing to do with the question of proof of guilt or innocence. Nor has any other part of this biography."

"Please approach." Benson was cold as ice. "Charley," he said to Anderson very softly, "you are behaving like an asshole, if you will forgive my choice of words, Ms. Ridley. This woman in the witness chair is on trial for her life, and I am going to give Ms. Ridley here every latitude. Let me explain something to you. The crime specified in 157 is not like breaking and entering. It is an action born out of a hundred different pressures, and I want the jury to hear all of these pressures that the defense desires to present. Do you understand me?"

"Yes, Your Honor."

And to Button, "Ms. Ridley, I leave it to your good sense to keep your examination within sensible boundaries."

"I will try, Your Honor."

"All right. Then let's get on with this damn trial!"

Button walked across, closer to the witness, and said, "Professor Goodman, you were saying that you feared for the lives of your children—or perhaps I am putting words in your mouth. I don't want to lead you."

"Yes, I feared for their lives."

"Only because of Mr. Haberman's beating?"

"No—no . . ." She hesitated. "I knew this town as a little girl. It's different today."

"How is it different?"

"It's filled with fear and anger—"

Anderson could not resist the impulse to rise. The judge fixed his gaze on him, and Anderson's objection died in a whisper.

"Professor Goodman," Button said, "during the years when your children were small, did you ever have permanent household help?"

"No—apart from the occasional baby-sitters. I raised my children at home. My husband had a small, struggling law business. When both my children were in grade school, I was able to resume my studies and get my doctorate in history."

"What was the title and subject of your dissertation—one moment before you answer." She turned to the jury. "The doctorate we are discussing here is the postgraduate degree of doctor of philosophy, a witness to a student's studies and abilities, not simply in philosophy; it can be in any discipline, as well as in medicine or dentistry. So you see, even though her subject was history, she is still called a doctor of philosophy." She turned back to Abigail.

"Yes, history was the subject. But I called my dissertation *The Invisible Woman*."

214

"Oh? A strange title. Why did you choose it?"

"Because I felt that to a certain degree, the role of women had been left out of history."

"I see. Now, Professor Goodman, when both your children were in school, as I understand it, you resumed your studies at Hilden College. Were you there simply as a student?"

"No. While working for my doctorate, I was taken on as an instructor. After I earned my degree, I became a part of the teaching faculty, and eventually, some five years ago, I became a tenured professor."

"By tenured, what exactly do you mean?"

"Having certain rights and privileges, not to be laid off without specific cause. It's an academic term, but of great importance to a teacher."

"I see. How important was this academic work to you?"

"It became, in a certain way, the central focus of my life. I felt, when my children were infants, that the most important contribution I could make was to raise two healthy children in a happy and functioning household."

"And do you feel, looking back, that yours was a happy and functioning household?"

"I felt that, yes."

"And was it enough? Did it satisfy you entirely?"

Abigail hesitated, then said, "No, it did not satisfy me entirely. Just as my husband could do more than being a father, I felt that without diminishing the care and love I gave my children, I was capable of something more."

"Something? What do you mean by that?"

215

"I am not belittling the skill and patience it takes to raise children and create a home. My husband was a lawyer during those years. If someone had come to him and said, Here is a judgeship if you want it, he could have accepted. I was not in that position. My children were first. I did tutoring, which I could do at home, and I took night courses while my husband sat with the children. When my children were finally at school, I was in a position to join the faculty at Hilden College. I had achieved something I had dreamed of."

Anderson could contain himself no longer. "I must object. We are being treated to a biography of the accused. Where is the connection? Where is the crime she is accused of?"

"You're overruled," Benson said flatly. "This goes to the alleged crime, so you'll have to simply stay with it, Mr. Anderson, and in due time you'll have your turn at cross-examination." He went on to say to Button, "I would hope, Ms. Ridley, that all this leads to something concrete."

"Yes, Your Honor, it will. Nevertheless, my client is charged with murder, and she has agreed to surrender her privilege and take the stand, an act of integrity—"

"That will be enough!" Benson snapped. "You will confine yourself to questioning the witness."

"Yes, Your Honor. I am sorry." She turned back to Abigail. "Professor Goodman, what were your plans for this forthcoming semester at Hilden College?"

"Well, I had convinced Professor Quigley, the head of the History Department, that while numerous attempts at the revision of historical data to include the role of women have been made, and while there was no shortage of monographs and biographical studies of women and their place in history, there was no course given, so far as I could determine, in the whole panorama of history as seen from the woman's point of view— that is, history as created by women as opposed to history created by men. I felt it would be an extraordinary achievement if such a course could be realized at Hilden."

"And do you believe that there is such a thing as history created by women?"

Anderson rose with his objection and threw up his arms in despair.

"Approach," Benson said tiredly, and when they stood before him, he said to Button, "Ms. Ridley, I decided to give you all the latitude the law would permit, but you have gone very far afield. I have no idea what you are aiming for with this notion of history created by women."

"Neither do I," Anderson said.

"I am going to sustain Mr. Anderson's objection. Ms. Ridley, you know the rules of evidence. Try to remember them."

"This is not your usual case, Your Honor."

"Really?"

"If you will grant me just a modicum of leeway, I think we can finish with the testimony of Professor Goodman this morning."

The judge then said to Anderson, "Suppose we both agree to do that, Mr. Anderson. Ms. Ridley is not leading the witness, nor is she impugning any of the testimony of your witnesses. If there was a character witness on the stand instead of the defendant, we would give her the same leeway. As I see it, Professor

Goodman is establishing a background picture of her life and motivations. She has not gone into true violation. Will you agree?"

Anderson nodded and went back to his table.

Button said to Abigail, "Let us continue on another course, Professor Goodman. As I understand it, you were living in Hilden as a child?"

"Yes, my father, Leon Henderson, practiced law at Blakely, a town about twenty miles from Hilden. He preferred to live in Hilden. Among other things, he taught an undergraduate course in contract law at Hilden College. Hilden has no law school."

"I see. You were Leon Henderson's only child?"

"Yes."

"And how old were you when he died?"

"I was nine years old. My mother had to go to work to make ends meet. She managed during the school months, but when summer came, there was simply no way she could care for me, and that was when my grandparents convinced her to send me here to Clarkton, to be with them through the summer months. At first I was very lonely and perhaps more deeply traumatized by my father's death than any believed me to be. But my grandparents were very kind to me, and I not only came to love them deeply, but to love this town as well."

"As I remember," Button said, "they lived in that big old Victorian house on Henderson Way?"

"Yes."

"And after your grandmother's death, the house was sold? Is that so?"

"Yes. My husband and I tried to keep it, but we didn't have the money to repair it. We sold it to Crompton Brothers, who tore it down to build the new shopping center. The old house was terribly dilapidated. There was no way we could re-pair it."

"I understand. And would you state why you were here in Clarkton when you were arrested?"

"Simply to finish signing the papers concerning the sale. Also, I wanted to see the old house again. We were too late. It had already been bulldozed."

"Yes. Now about those summer months you spent with your grandparents, how many summers were there?"

"I spent six summers with my grandparents."

"Ah, yes. Were they happy summers?"

"The happiest time of my childhood. My grandparents were wonderful people. My grandfather was a great attorney, a man who defended the poor and the oppressed—"

Anderson was on his feet, complaining that since her grand-father was not on trial, he hardly needed a character witness.

"I do hope we are coming to the end of this line of question-ing," Benson said.

"Very close to the end, Your Honor," Button said. "Now tell me, Professor Goodman, during those wonderful summer months you spent with your grandparents, you were an active child, were you not?"

"I did what kids do. I swam in the old pond. I walked into town for ice-cream sodas. I read a great deal. I listened to music with my grandparents—"

"Of course. And since you appear to have been an active child, you had your share of cuts and scratches."

"I did."

"Anything worse than cuts and scratches?"

"Once. I was eleven, and I tried to slide down the bannister of the front staircase. I lost my balance and tumbled off and fractured my arm."

"Really. Anything else?"

"Yes, one summer I had a very bad strep throat. My temperature went up to a hundred and four and scared my poor grandparents to death—"

"No, this is too much!" Anderson cried. "I must object!"

"Really, Ms. Ridley," the judge said. "Are we to have a catalog of every cut and bruise your client suffered? Can you somehow return this to the matter at hand?"

"I have only two or three questions more, if Your Honor will allow me?"

"Very well. I am denying your objection, Mr. Anderson. We'll both have patience."

"A broken arm," Button said. "One hundred and four degrees of fever—that is serious stuff, wouldn't you say, Professor Goodman?"

"It goes with being a child."

"But it calls for the doctor, doesn't it?"

220

"Absolutely."

"And did your grandparents call a doctor?"

"They certainly did."

"And who was this doctor? What was his name?"

"Doctor Jason Briggs. He was a wonderful old man. He had a white goatee, a white mustache, and he wore a black cutaway coat. He was an old southern gentleman, just as courtly as could be."

"Does he still practice in Clarkton?"

"Heavens, no. He died about twenty years ago."

"Did your grandparents ever call any other doctor to attend to whatever might have ailed you? Did they ever call Dr. Raymond Sykes?"

"No, they wouldn't have dreamed of it."

"Of course not, when they could have a fine old gentleman like Doctor Jason Briggs in their home!" Button now turned to the bench and said, "I am through with this witness, Your Honor."

"Through with her?"

"Yes, I have no more questions."

Benson stared at Button for a long moment, shook his head ever so slightly, and then said, "Very well."

Anderson and his assistants stared in amazement, whispered among themselves—and the whispers flooded the courtroom until Benson tapped for silence.

Only at the table for the defense was there no whispering. They sat smugly quiet and relaxed, the Ridleys, William Goodman, and Jim Cooper, the law student.

"Mr. Anderson," the judge said, "I presume you will have cross-examination for this witness?"

"Yes, Your Honor."

"It is already well past noon. I suggest we break for lunch and convene again at half-past one."

July 24. Eileen Mott, special to the *New York Globe:*

To the amazement of everyone at today's trial of Abigail Goodman, Professor Goodman herself took the stand. She testified through the morning, and I am filing this brief report during the lunch hour break. The examination of the witness was undertaken by Ms. Button Ridley, who proved so brilliant in her examination of Dr. Steven Burger.

I cannot say the same of her examination of Abigail Goodman. It ranged over the life and background of Professor Goodman and was as far from the question at hand as an examination might be. The people in the courtroom sat in expectant silence, waiting for Professor Goodman to denounce the proceedings and to tear the People's case to shreds, but alas, the mountain gave forth a mouse, and we were treated to a sort of sound-bite biography of Professor Goodman that led up to no more than the cuts and scratches she had received playing as a child in her grandparents' home in Clarkton.

Along with the other correspondents, I found the examination by Ms. Ridley to be inexplicable. Why she put Abigail Goodman on the witness stand I cannot for the life of me imagine, nor have I spoken to anyone who has a reasonable explanation. I must say, however, that both Ms. Goodman and the defense team seem totally undisturbed by the morning's proceedings. They refused to answer any questions or to make any comments on the process. Possibly this afternoon's session will throw some light on the matter. I must say that I sincerely hope so. Professor Goodman is a brave and admirable woman, and she deserves the best defense in this strange and unhappy matter.

14

THERE WAS NO straggling into the courtroom. At half-past one, it was packed full, the general pretrial noise muted to whispers. The judge entered and Abigail took her place on the witness chair.

"Professor Goodman, you are still under oath," the judge reminded her.

Anderson could not help but strut a bit as he took up a position facing Abigail. After asking her age and place of residence, he said, "What was the date of your abortion?"

Abigail regarded him mildly without replying. Button rose and said, "Objection."

"Oh? On what grounds?" Benson asked.

"It's a road we never traveled. Mr. Anderson is engaged in cross-examination of a hostile witness, our witness. I never touched on the question of abortion, and I never mentioned abortion."

"What about that, Mr. Anderson?" the judge asked.

"Of course she mentioned abortion!"

"I can have the whole record of my examination of Professor Goodman read back, but that will take time, Your Honor."

"As my memory serves me, Mr. Anderson," the judge said, "Ms. Ridley is right. She never mentioned abortion. I'm going to support her objection."

"Exception!" Anderson said angrily.

"So noted," Benson said.

Anderson went back to his table and conferred with his colleagues. Then he returned to face Abigail and said, "Professor Goodman, did you ever have elective surgery?"

Again Button rose to object. She and Anderson were both on their feet, facing the bench, making their arguments. Benson held up his hands. "Enough!" he snapped. "Will both of you please be silent."

They stood in front of him while he studied them thoughtfully. Finally he said, "In my chambers."

In his office, Benson dropped onto his desk chair and left both Button and Anderson standing. "I have not had a decent night of sleep since this case began, and neither of you do anything to help. I'm beginning to see the path you're following,

Ms. Ridley, and I'm beginning to understand Abigail Good-man's testimony today."

"I thought you would, Your Honor," Button said.

"That kind of apple polishing will get you nowhere."

"Would someone enlighten me?" Anderson asked.

"Ms. Ridley," the judge said, "your intention, I presume, is to prevent Mrs. Goodman from answering any questions pertaining to the alleged abortion. Is that the case?"

"Yes. No doors were opened on that subject."

"Yet it goes to the heart of the crime," Anderson argued. "This is preposterous!"

"Yes and no," Benson said. "Suppose, Ms. Ridley, I instruct your client that she must answer Mr. Anderson's questions?"

"Then I will advise her to take the Fifth Amendment against self-incrimination."

"But she surrendered her privilege!" Anderson exclaimed. "The moment she took the witness stand, she surrendered her privilege."

"Yes and no," Benson said. "She still retains the right not to incriminate herself. You are going to quote the *State of California* versus *Patricia Hearst*—am I right, Ms. Ridley?"

"I have seven other citations," Button said. "Patty Hearst is simply the most notorious."

"What in hell does Patty Hearst have to do with all this?" Anderson demanded.

"She surrendered her privilege, Mr. Anderson," the judge said. "You should remember that. She also selectively took the

Fifth Amendment. It was upheld." He turned back to Button. "I could hold your witness in contempt—"

"Possibly."

"You subpoenaed another witness today," Benson began.

Anderson exploded. "How? What kind of game is she playing?"

"I am terribly sorry," Button said humbly. "Please, Mr. Anderson, I should have informed you immediately, but it was only this morning, only this morning—believe me, please."

"And you authorized this subpoena?" Anderson demanded of the judge. "You authorized it without my knowledge?"

"Just pull yourself together, Charley," Benson said with annoyance. "A copy of the subpoena is sitting on your table. Either one of your boys opened it and didn't think it important enough to pass on, or you just let it sit there."

"Who is this witness?" Anderson muttered.

"Dr. Raymond Sykes."

"Sykes?"

"That's right."

"And you're going to support her objections?" Anderson demanded.

"I think so," Benson said gravely. "It's a lot simpler and cleaner than getting into the Fifth Amendment stuff. I don't think you want a constitutional issue in there. Do you, Charley?"

"The hell with it," Anderson said. "I don't need her. It was a piece of idiocy putting her on the stand in the first place."

"I'm glad you feel that way," Benson said.

They returned to the courtroom, where Abigail still sat on the witness stand.

"I have no more questions for this witness," Anderson said.

As Benson leaned over to tell Abigail she could step down, Button said, "Please, Your Honor, I have a few questions for my witness as redirect."

Benson sighed. "Very well, Ms. Ridley."

"Professor Goodman," Button said slowly, "I am going to ask you a number of questions. You might be inclined to answer them quickly. I want you to give each question a bit more than a moment's thought. Now to begin: Have you ever heard the name Dr. Raymond Sykes—that is, before I asked about him in your direct testimony?"

"Yes."

"Under what circumstances have you heard this name?"

"At a meeting of my attorneys, when they decided to call him as a witness."

"When was that?"

"The day after the assault on Carl Haberman, the day this trial was suspended for twenty-four hours."

"Did you ever see Dr. Raymond Sykes?"

"No, I did not."

"Would you recognize him if you saw him?"

"No, I would not."

"He is present in this courtroom. Can you pick him out and identify him?"

"No, I cannot."

"Did you ever speak to him on the telephone?"

"No, I did not."

"Did you ever have a letter, note, or any other kind of communication from him?"

"No, I did not."

"Did you ever make any attempt to communicate in any way, by voice or note or telephone or fax, with Dr. Raymond Sykes?"

"No, I did not."

"Did you ever go to his office?"

"No, I did not."

"Did you ever meet him under any circumstances?"

"No, I did not."

"Do you know where his office is?"

"No, I do not."

"He has a receptionist, name of Letty Jones, and a nurse, name of Clara Bennett. Do you know either of them?"

"No, I do not."

"Thank you, Professor." She turned to a frowning Benson. "I have no other questions for this witness."

"You may step down," Benson said to Abigail, meanwhile motioning Button to join him. Anderson also approached the bench.

"It is almost two-thirty," Benson said. "You have nine other witnesses scheduled, Ms. Ridley. What are you intentions?"

"I would like to call Dr. Sykes."

"Can you finish with him this afternoon?"

"I think so."

"Then let's get to it."

Anderson returned to his table and began a hasty whispered

conversation with his colleagues. The clerk called, "Dr. Raymond Sykes to the stand!" Button went to her table and took a long drink of water. Dr. Raymond Sykes walked up the aisle and took his place on the witness stand. He was a slender man of medium height, hair set in a tasteful wave, glasses on a black ribbon around his neck, erect, making a statement to the effect that his fifty-five years or so were still on the better side of middle age.

Button watched Dr. Sykes being sworn in, and then she took a binder containing several sheets of paper, handed it to Benson, and asked that it be entered as evidence. She had two copies, one of which she gave to Anderson. His response was immediate and angry.

"I cannot accept this!" Anderson cried, spluttering as he tried to find the right words. "I object vigorously."

"This is a sworn deposition," Benson said. "You have no reason to object."

"We have no confirmation."

"We have a witness on the stand," Benson said. "The deposition simply spells out a statement the witness is said to have made. You will have the witness's answers on the record."

"I would like to read the deposition to the jury," Button said.

"I object to that. Damn it, Your Honor, I object to that."

Benson motioned the lawyers to approach, and Abigail could have sworn that he was trying to keep the corners of his mouth from twitching. He said to Button softly, "I know what you are going to quote me, Ms. Ridley. There were those very famous trials, the People versus an infamous Mafia family, where tapes were played with the voices of the defendants. But you see, they were on trial, so that they could claim the privilege of not testifying personally. Dr. Sykes is not on trial. Ask him the questions directly. He is under oath, and he will testify personally. As for this deposition, I would like to hold it in abeyance until you have finished with your witness."

"And your intentions at that point, Your Honor?" Anderson demanded. "Will you accept it as evidence or not?"

"Don't push me, Charley. We are all in one hell of a crisis. So don't push me. When the time comes, I'll decide, and no one else. I swear to God, I don't know who's in more trouble, you or that quack on the witness stand. Or myself, for that matter."

"Can we speak in chambers?" Anderson wanted to know.

"No!" The judge's whisper came like a hiss. "We will not talk in chambers. I want to hear what this witness has to say."

"Can I use this deposition to get a yes or no response from the witness?" Button asked.

"Goddamn it, no!" Anderson whispered.

"Charley," the judge said very softly, "shut up! Let's get on with this crazy trial."

Every reporter in attendance was scribbling wildly as Button took her position in front of the witness box, the deposition in her hand. "What is your name?" she asked Sykes.

"Raymond Sykes, M.D."

"Ah, Raymond indeed," Button said. "M.D. And where did you go to medical school, Dr. Raymond?"

"Dr. Sykes, if you please."

"Of course. Dr. Sykes. Medical school?"

"Johns Hopkins."

"Worthy school. How do they teach the Hippocratic oath? I've often wondered. Do they hand you flyers as gifts, or do they ask you to memorize it?"

Dr. Sykes sat silent.

"Not an important question. Let the record show—"

"I didn't get the question, Ms. Ridley," the stenographer said.

"I asked the good doctor whether they handed out copies of the Hippocratic oath to put in their wallets, or whether students had to memorize it."

Anderson was rising to his feet.

"You know better than that, Ms. Ridley," Benson said, and to the stenographer, "Forget it. Not in the record."

"Dr. Sykes," Button said, her tone cold and nasty, "you were in court half an hour ago when Professor Goodman was on the witness stand and I asked her a series of questions in redirect examination. Is that not so?"

"Yes."

"You were sitting in the rear row on the left, in the three-seat section reserved for witnesses. Is that not so?"

"Yes."

"And you could hear all of her testimony?"

"Yes, I suppose so."

"Now I remind you that you are under oath. Is Professor Goodman a patient of yours?"

Dr. Raymond Sykes struggled with the question. He looked at the judge and he looked at Anderson, and he found no comfort in either place.

"No," he finally replied.

"Was she ever a patient?"

"No."

"Has she ever asked you for medical attention of any kind?"

"No."

"Has she ever set foot in your office?"

"No."

"Now, on or about May tenth, did you make a telephone call to Dr. Arthur Campbell at Hilden Hospital? And before you answer, I am reminding you that this was a long-distance call and as such was put on the record."

"Yes."

"Would you please tell the jury who Dr. Arthur Campbell is?"

"He's chief of surgery at Hilden Hospital."

"Good, good. We progress. Now, did you not tell Dr. Campbell that you were Professor Goodman's personal physician?"

"Yes," after a long, long pause.

"And that was a lie, was it not?"

After a struggle with himself and a beseeching look at Anderson, "Yes."

"Did the decision to tell that lie originate with you?"

"No," he said hopelessly.

"Then who told you to do what you did?"

Dr. Sykes struggled with this. Then he turned to Benson and asked, "Must I answer that question?"

"Yes."

"And if I don't choose to, Your Honor?"

"If you refuse to, Dr. Sykes, I will hold you in contempt and put you in jail, and there you will stay until you purge yourself of contempt by answering the question."

"I can't do that," Sykes said miserably. "I have patients. I have sick people who depend on me."

"Then answer the question," Benson said.

Dr. Sykes struggled for hope and reprieve, turned to Anderson and then again to the judge, and found nothing in either place.

"Are you telling me that this was your own idea?" Button asked in disgust.

"No—well, yes, in a way—"

"All right," Button said. "We begin again. Why did you telephone Dr. Campbell and state to him that you were Professor Goodman's physician?"

"In order for him to send me the records of her abortion."

"And you accomplished this by pretending to be Professor Goodman's physician, is that not so?"

"Yes."

"Very well. Now, why did you perpetrate this deception?"

Dr. Sykes took a long breath, clenched his fists, and said, "I knew Mr. Anderson wanted a test of section 157 here in Clarkton. I knew he hoped to be a candidate for the United States Senate in the fall, and I heard him mention how much a trial based on the new abortion statute might mean to him in the way of publicity."

"What do you mean, you heard him mention? How did he mention this? Where did he mention it?"

"I had lunch with him about another matter."

"Tell us about that other matter, Dr. Sykes."

Anderson was on his feet, objecting angrily.

Benson said, "I am going to sustain the district attorney's objection. I do not see how this other matter is pertinent to the business at hand. Dr. Sykes is your witness, not Mr. Anderson's."

Button nodded, turned back to Dr. Sykes, appeared unable to shake her expression of disgust, and asked him, "And was it Mr. Anderson's notion that you pretend to be the professor's physician?"

Sykes hesitated before he admitted, "No. I had already obtained the record."

"On your own? What an unusual physician you are! But why? Did you know that Professor Goodman was coming here?"

"Yes. Ralph Crompton bought the Henderson property—he's a patient of mine—he mentioned that Professor Goodman was due down here to close the deal, but that some minor surgery had delayed her arrival and the deal."

"Whereupon you called Hilden Hospital and obtained her records under false pretenses. Is that not so?"

He nodded.

"Please answer for the record!" Button snapped.

"Yes."

"What an astonishing physician you are, Dr. Raymond Sykes!"

"Do I have to sit here and listen to her insults?" he demanded of Benson.

"I'm afraid you do," the judge said.

"And then," Button said relentlessly, "upholding your Hippocratic oath and your honor as a southern gentleman, you called the district attorney and informed him that you had something real rich, that he might use to hang Professor Goodman by the neck. Is that not so?"

"Not that way—no."

"What way, then?"

"I was doing my duty."

"Bless your foul heart!"

Anderson was on his feet. Judge Benson cried, "I will not have this kind of thing in my court! You know that, Ms. Ridley! Once more and I'll hold you in contempt."

"Oh, I am so sorry. Forgive me," Button begged him.

"Her last statement is off the record," he told the stenographer.

Button turned back to her witness. "And how much of this deception did Mr. Anderson know about? Did you tell him you were Professor Goodman's physician?"

Another pleading look at Anderson, and then, "Well, sort of."

"Yes or no."

"Well—I let him think so."

"But she lived in Hilden and you practiced here. Why should Mr. Anderson have believed you?"

"He believed me." He hesitated.

"Go on, sir. I want you to tell me how you convinced Dr. Campbell in Hilden to send you Professor Goodman's records, and I want you to tell me how you convinced Mr. Anderson that Professor Goodman was your patient."

Dr. Sykes had begun, as Button put it afterward, to come

apart at the seams. He mopped his brow, chewed his lower lip, and blinked rapidly. Button gave him no space.

"Doctor," she said, "I want to hear an answer. I asked you a question. Please answer it."

"I invented a story," Sykes admitted.

"Did you? Tell us about it."

"I told Dr. Campbell that Professor Goodman was here in Clarkton and suffered from an endometritis."

"Suppose you explain that to the jury. What is an endometritis?"

"An inflammation of the uterus. It can happen after an abortion."

"I see. That was your lie to Dr. Campbell at Hilden Hospital. Now, doctor, tell us about your lie to Mr. Anderson—if indeed what you told him was a lie. What did you tell him?"

"The same thing."

"What same thing? Please be specific and tell me exactly what you told Mr. Anderson."

"I told him that after having had the abortion at Hilden Hospital, Professor Goodman came to me with an endometritis."

"You are under oath, doctor! Think! What did you tell Mr. Anderson?"

"Exactly what I said I told him."

Button walked away from him, shaking her head. She paused to look at Anderson, but he avoided her gaze. She walked to the jury box and regarded the jurors hopelessly—as if words failed where Sykes was concerned. Then she turned and stared thoughtfully at Dr. Sykes. Minutes ticked past.

Benson said, "Ms. Ridley, do you propose to continue with your examination? Time is passing. If not, I must ask the district attorney to cross-examine."

"I have a few more questions."

"Then please continue."

"Dr. Sykes," Button said almost absently, "do you do abortions?"

"Objection," Anderson said almost tentatively, the steam gone out of him.

"What are you up to, Ms. Ridley?" Benson said with annoyance. "Have you any reason to attack the witness with an accusation like this?"

"I did not attack him. I simply asked him a question. He's a physician. At least he says he is. That's a perfectly natural question."

"I'm sustaining the objection. You will not answer that question," Benson said to Sykes.

"Very well," Button said. "You have explained how you obtained the records of Ms. Goodman's surgery at Hilden Hospital—through fraud and deception. Fraud and deception and invention—is that not true, Dr. Sykes?"

"Well, now—"

"Well now, nothing!" Button snorted, advancing on him. "I asked you a question. Answer yes or no!"

"Yes."

"And is it true that you then turned over these records to Mr. Anderson?"

"Yes."

"And the records became the basis for the arrest and indictment of Professor Abigail Goodman, is that not so?"

He was slow to answer this. "I don't know."

"Of course you know. What other reason was there for turning them over to Mr. Anderson?"

"I don't know."

"So you don't know," Button said in disgust, and turning to the judge, "I have nothing more for this creature."

"You may step down," Benson said to Dr. Sykes. "You will not leave this jurisdiction until some legal determination of your conduct is made." And turning to the district attorney, "As for you, Mr. Anderson, you will join Ms. Ridley in my chambers."

"I would like Mr. Ridley and Mr. Goodman to be with me," Button said.

"As you wish." He turned to the jury. "The jury is dismissed for the day. Court will convene at ten o'clock tomorrow morning."

July 21. Dede Brown, National Public Radio:

The spectators in the courthouse in Clarkton, USA, where Professor Abigail Goodman faces a death sentence if convicted of having an abortion after the first trimester of her pregnancy, were treated today to an absolutely amazing demonstration of venality and dishonesty. As in every case where a law singles out a minority or an already oppressed segment of the population, common decency on the part of the oppressor is thrown to the wind.

The testimony today of Dr. Raymond Sykes, a local physician here in Clarkton, put forward the following facts: first, that the evidence upon which Professor Goodman was arrested was tainted evidence, spurious and obtained under false pretenses; and second, that the district attorney prosecuting Professor Goodman for the People, one Charles Anderson by name, had connived in the presentation of this tainted evidence.

Upon receiving this information, Judge Benson, whose behavior has been almost meticulously correct under these trying conditions, summarily dismissed the jury for the day and stated that he would receive both the prosecution and the defense in his chambers.

Rumors are rife wherever one turns in this town that was catapulted so suddenly into world notoriety, and everyone I spoke to has a legal opinion. Myself, I prefer to wait until ten o'clock tomorrow morning to hear what Judge Benson makes of all this. I must mention that while Judge Benson has the reputation of being a tough and unsympathetic jurist, given to long sentences for drug dealers and using the death sentence three times for murders committed in the drug trade, he is nevertheless respected for his fairness and his integrity. There is little doubt as to why the chief justice of the state chose him to hear this case. Aware that number 157 of the penal code of the state was bound to cause anger and opposition in many quarters, both here and abroad, they put their best foot forward with

Judge Benson, knowing that he would follow the law to its bitter end.

Putting Abigail Goodman on the witness stand today is now more understandable, not only to flesh out her character, but to prove that Dr. Raymond Sykes's claim to be her physician was absolutely false. I must confess that I expected Button Ridley to dwell on possible hazards in allowing a woman past her forty-first year to carry a pregnancy to term. However, she chose instead to present Professor Goodman as a very normal, ordinary woman who decided, after her children were grown and off to college, that she was entitled to a career of her own.

I must mention that Button Ridley, the litigator today, is a totally disarming and unassuming woman. With her round face, her soft gray-blue eyes, and her graying brown hair, she looks for all the world like someone's favorite grandmother, withal a youthful one. As two of the witnesses learned, she can be very dangerous.

15

IN HIS CHAMBERS, sitting behind his desk and bleakly observing the four lawyers, Benson said, "Well, Charley, what have you got to say for yourself?"

Anderson had worked up sufficient courage to muster a defense. He tried to be casual, wiping his gold-rimmed glasses and shrugging. "I knew a crime had been committed, and I went about collecting evidence. May I smoke, Your Honor?" He had the pack of cigarettes in his hand.

"You may not!"

"But I did not suborn evidence. That son of a bitch is lying."

242

"I don't believe you," Benson said shortly. "You wanted evidence, and you suborned a witness and turned him into a liar."

"He told me he was her physician. God Almighty, Judge, I believed him."

"What did you have on him? Was he doing illegal abortions?"

"I resent that."

"Resent it all the way to hell if you wish. Charley, let me tell you something. In all my years on the bench, I have not encountered another horse's ass like you. Do you know what you have done? You have tainted the evidence beyond repair. You are neck deep in shit!" He turned to Button. "I beg your pardon, Ms. Ridley. The language is unpleasant, but it applies. I think you and your team did a good job. Frankly, I think the jury would have found your client innocent."

He turned back to Anderson. "But we'll never know that, will we, Charley? The one matter of proof that does not exist at this moment is any evidence that Professor Goodman ever had an abortion. It is tainted and worthless. It was obtained by deceit and subornation, and it puts me in the position where, as a matter of law, I must direct a verdict of innocence. You rested your case, and Professor Goodman cannot be tried again. That would be double jeopardy. Tomorrow morning, I am going to discharge the jury and inform Professor Goodman that she is free to leave. As far as you and Dr. Sykes are concerned, I will decide what to do and whether to bring charges and what charges to bring."

"I swear to God I didn't know he was lying," Anderson pleaded.

Benson said, "Go home and explain to your wife why you will no longer continue as district attorney of this county." When Anderson continued to stand in front of him, Judge Benson said, "You can go, Charley. I've said what I have to say. If you figure me to be a mean bastard, so be it. You made your own grief. Don't blame me."

His face set as grimly as a chubby man's face could be set, Anderson left, slamming the door behind him. Benson studied the three lawyers who stood facing him.

"Sit down," he said abruptly.

They seated themselves, and Benson opened the drawer of his desk and took out a cigar, matches, and an ashtray. While they watched him, he took a small cutter out of his waistcoat pocket, cut the cigar, and inhaled with pleasure.

"No, I would not let that little son of a bitch smoke a cigarette here. I don't like him and I don't like cigarettes. A good cigar is something else entirely. Well, Ridley, how do you feel?"

"Like I have been put through hell."

"Goodman, I do hope that after tomorrow you're not going to run?"

"Run? Where?" said Bill.

"Out of state. Away from the local barbarians."

There was a knock at the door. Then it opened, and a court attendant said, "I got Professor Goodman standing out here. She wants to know whether she should stay or return to the hotel."

"Tell her to come in," the judge said, and when Abigail entered, he said, "Please sit down. I've just told your counsel that I'm going to wind up this trial tomorrow with a directed verdict of not guilty. I think you understand why. All evidence linking you to an abortion is tainted."

Abigail scarcely dared say it. "Do you mean the trial is over? I'm free?"

"Exactly."

Abigail rose, went to her husband and kissed him, and then went to Button and embraced her. She was crying. Jack Ridley watched her intently. She had not cried like this before. She went to Ridley and kissed him.

Benson smoked his cigar with pleasure. "In the morning," he said to Abigail. "You'll have to appear in court in the morning."

"Yes, I understand."

Bill gave her his handkerchief, and she wiped away the tears.

"I was asking your husband whether, after going through all of this, you intend to leave the state?"

"But I live here," Abigail said.

"Yes, you do," Benson said. "I remember your granddaddy. We produce a round number of sons of bitches, but we also produce some pretty decent specimens. It's a good place to live. The climate is fine, and the way most people live, they never know what they can do until it's put to them."

Abigail nodded.

"You going to go on teaching?"

"They said they'd hold my job for me, even if I went to prison," Abigail managed through her tears.

"It may be a little harder for these three lawyers you hired, but the way things are going down at the capital, business will pick up. Don't ever sell us short, Miss Abigail. I'll see you all in court in the morning."

At ten o'clock the following morning, after the audience in the courtroom had been called to order, Judge Benson entered and took his seat on the bench. After studying the assembled audience, the people in the jury box, the group around Charles Anderson, the group at the table for the defense, the packed rows of correspondents, and all the rest who filled the courtroom, he cleared his throat and said, "Since yesterday, I have reviewed the evidence presented here, and I have studied the question of Abigail Goodman's guilt or innocence under section 157 of the criminal code. The State has brought forward no witness who was eyewitness to the alleged abortion of which Professor Goodman is accused. The single piece of circumstantial evidence upon which the People's case was based are the records of an abortion at Hilden Hospital, but this single piece of evidence was obtained by conspiratorial deceit and is therefore tainted and cannot be accepted as evidence. Thus the People have failed to make a prima facie case as a matter of law. Since the stricture against double jeopardy in capital punishment applies in this case, the People cannot present a new indictment and place Abigail Goodman on trial once again. I have no alternative but to declare the prisoner at the bar not guilty, and she is free to go. The jury is dismissed with the thanks of the court for their patience."

July 22. Eileen Mott, special to the *New York Globe:*

The extraordinary decision of Judge George Lee Benson in this case of the *State* against *Professor Abigail Goodman* was not only unexpected, but a true blessing for the Goodmans. I have already heard snorts of annoyance from those who felt that it was almost a patriotic duty on the part of Professor Goodman to be convicted, so that the case might go on to the Supreme Court of the United States. But anyone who has watched the composition of the high court change during the past years must realize that there would have been little hope of the Supreme Court reversing section 157 of this state's criminal code. Certainly the Goodmans were understandably delighted with the decision, and it is to be expected, according to the two local state senators I have spoken to, that the worldwide notoriety given this case might even lead to the overturning of the statute here in this state. One of the two senators I spoke with told me that no one in the state legislature had anticipated such international interest and condemnation. They had expected support from Washington, but no such support was forthcoming.

There is a movement in the state to place Judge Benson in nomination for governor in the upcoming election, and the same senator I spoke to said, somewhat cynically, that Judge Benson was waiting for the opportunity to direct a verdict, and that if the testimony of Dr. Sykes had not appeared, he would have devised some other excuse to end the trial. He also assured me that the sitting governor, at the state capital, has already selected Charles Anderson, the district attorney, as their sacrificial lamb. But as far as I can see, no tears are being shed for Mr. Anderson, and the weight of opinion is that both he and Dr. Sykes face criminal charges. The bandwagon that voted section 157 into existence is beginning to shift course, and more people are jumping off each day.

The defense team held their press conference at three o'clock of that same day, in the packed dining room of the Jackson House, the largest local hotel. Of course, the first questions to Professor Goodman went to her state of mind, and she expressed relief and joy at the verdict.

"At the same time," she said, "I must tell you that after the initial fears, I had composed myself to the point of accepting the possibility of a guilty verdict, and then fighting it through to the Supreme Court."

A question to Jack Ridley, chief of the defense team: "Mr. Ridley, do you believe that there will be other trials?"

"I hope not. I know that other trials were planned—but perhaps the events here in Clarkton may dampen the enthusiasm of the governor."

Mr. Conte Laponi, correspondent of the Italian paper *Avanti,* asked, "What is your future, your plans, Professor?"

"To go home and resume my work."

"Are you not afraid?"

"We live in a world where being afraid is quite a normal thing. One lives with it."

"But in my country, in Italy, when Mussolini became dictator most important intellectuals fled or were imprisoned."

"But this is not Italy or Germany."

"But it is the South, Professor," Laponi insisted.

"Yes, and right here in the South, I was tried and freed."

I managed to get a question in. "What is the attitude of your university people?"

"As I've said, my job is still there."

"And you will not change the text of your course?"

"Absolutely not."

"Do you think it might have been better for the country if the case had gone to the jury?"

"Possibly. What it would have done to me, I can't say."

Having watched the development and progress of the trial, this correspondent can say that she has only admiration for the courage and comportment of Professor Goodman.

July 22. Frank Geller, special to the *Chicago Times:*

The directed verdict by Judge George Lee Benson, which set Abigail Goodman free on the basis of tainted and inadmissible evidence, does not, in the judgment of this correspondent and many others, change the fact of Mrs. Goodman's guilt. The crowing and cheering by the National Organization for Women and similar feminist and Choice groups who flooded down here to Clarkton in their hired buses does not reflect the will or the spirit of this nation.

The big question, unanswered in this case, is what would have happened had this case gone to the jury? I took it on myself to interview each member of the jury after the jury was discharged. The jury consisted of eight men and four women. Two of the male members of the jury and one of the female members were black.

Norman Lotts, foreman of the jury, is an ex-policeman, and his comment to me was sharp and succinct. "That over-educated fancy bitch broke the law. She was as guilty as hell."

Joseph Biddle is a plumber's assistant. His wife is pregnant with their fifth child. Biddle is a mild man, broken in spirit, but when we talked about the judge's directed verdict, his anger surfaced. "My wife is carrying," he said. "You don't see me getting no abortion. If God didn't want this child to be born, He never would have made Hetty pregnant." There is no doubt in my mind how he would have voted.

Hasty Morgan is one of the white women, a widow living frugally on her Social Security check. Her comment was, "It's about time," referring to section 157 of the state's criminal code. "I got six children and eleven grandchildren. When I think of killing one of them, it just breaks me up into pieces." She's a born-again Christian.

Morris McGrath is a black man, a hospital orderly. He said, "Look, man, I work in the local hospital. That's where my bread is buttered. I got nothing else to say."

Georgia May Kent would not give a yes or no answer. She works as a stenographer at Liston & Gregory, a local law firm. She would only say, "The law's the law. I do work for lawyers."

Susan Sinclair is a clerk at a local insurance company. "They thought I had an abortion. Never did. Willie and me, we just keep trying." There's little doubt in my mind the way she would have voted.

Huey Mantel's an easygoing man in his forties who works as a cashier at the Piggly Wiggly. He made a great point of not wanting to do any harm to that "professor lady." "Trouble is," he said, "in a place like this . . . well, you sit on the jury and there ain't nobody won't know how you voted. I mean, sooner or later. A man's got to think about that."

Fred Ashton's an educated man. Rumor has it that he once taught at a fancy school upstate and that something happened between him and one of the kids at the school, but that's only a rumor, and he denies it vigorously. He runs the local bookstore, for want of a better name: newspapers, magazines, soft-cover books, greeting cards, and in back, magazines like *Playboy* and *Penthouse* and some porn tapes. I have been told that Charles Anderson, the district attorney, refuses to make an arrest and indict him. He refuses to answer any questions about the way he would have voted, but considering his friendship with Mr. Anderson, it's not hard to guess.

Oscar Butterfly is a black man in his forties who works as a short-order cook at Morton's Lunch Emporium. He refused to offer any information on how he would have voted. He said he never had a chance to make up his mind. But Toby Morton, the owner of the restaurant, tells me that Oscar knows the right time, and if word got around that he had voted to free the professor, it wouldn't make Clarkton a better place for him to live by any means.

Alice Johnson works at the Coca-Cola bottling plant. She is nineteen years old, a good-looking blonde. "Sure I felt for her," she told me, "but I got to live here and work here. My boyfriend calls her a lousy, stuck-up, upstate bitch, and he'd break my neck if word got out that I had hung the jury. I knew where they all stood. I'm no hero. Why should I be? I got to live here."

Hope Williams is a soprano in the choir at the First Baptist Church. She's a single woman in her early fifties. She said, "If you think I'm going to tell you, Mr. Newspaper Man, how I would have voted about that godless woman, you are just crazy."

The final member of the jury I interviewed was a black woman named Essie Lotus. "No, sir," she said. "I will not tell you how I would have voted. I prayed to God to give me some guidance. At the same time, when I see so many poor women willing to bear a child and work themselves to death raising it, and sometimes see it end up God only knows how and where . . . well, it does set me to thinking."

So much for the various members of the jury. This correspondent has no doubt that if the case had gone to the jury,

Professor Goodman would have ended up in a cell, waiting for the judge to pronounce sentence on her.

Driving home, from Clarkton to Hilden, the town where the Goodmans lived and where William Goodman practiced law and where Abigail Goodman would teach a course on women and history, Abigail sat and wept for over half an hour.

"I can't stop," she told her husband.

"Then don't stop. Let it all come out."

"I promised to drive part of the way," she said.

"Later. And when you do, I'll cry."

"You don't cry," she sobbed.

"That's what you think."

"Well, where do you cry if I don't see it?"

"In the bathroom."

"I don't believe that."

"It's the truth," he said.

"Everybody thinks I'm such a hero."

"Heroine, you mean."

"No, I don't," she sobbed. "I mean hero. I'm not a hero, but Jack Ridley says I am."

"You're wonderful," Bill said. "Why can't you be a heroine?"

"Because it's a put-down word, poetess, actress, sculptress—it puts us down and what we do and what we stand for."

"All right. You're a hero. I love you. You're wonderful."

"You're just saying that because I'm crying."

"I love you when you're not crying."

"Everyone thinks I'm someone else. Professor Abigail Goodman, strong, tough, unshakable. That's such bullshit. Do you know how it feels to think about being put to death by a hypodermic needle? I would lie awake at night and think about it, and Leon and Hope would be watching, the three of you standing there together and watching while their mother was stuck with a poisonous needle. Did you ever think about it?"

"I thought about it."

She managed to stop sobbing. "When?" The edge of anger was just beginning to show.

"Lying next to you. When you thought I was asleep, I wasn't asleep."

"You certainly were. You were snoring. You're my husband. How could you face what was going to happen to me?"

"I couldn't," he said miserably. "I couldn't face it at all. I hired a plane, a Lear corporate jet. I gave the pilot a certified check for ten thousand dollars. That was almost all we had in our partnership account, but Frank Brodsky said it was the right thing. He went along with it. The pilot is a bit shady, does some drug running. I got to him through Sam Bonoldi. You remember, I represented Bonoldi in the tape case and kept him out of jail. But he's okay—I mean, dependable according to his lights."

"Bill, are you crazy?"

"I kept thinking about you and that damn injection."

"You gave some drug runner ten thousand dollars?"

"I couldn't touch your money, the money you got for Granny's house and the money in our account."

She stopped crying and turned her tearstained face to him. "Let me understand this. This is not a joke?"

"Well, yes and no."

"What do you mean, yes and no?" she demanded.

"Well, it was dead serious when we set it up, but now it seems crazy."

"And exactly what were you going to do?"

"Well, the day the case went to the jury, I was going to get you into the plane and we'd fly to Mexico—and then Europe or something."

"And you thought I'd go—I'd run out on Jack and Button, and wreck your life and make it impossible for us ever to return home here and force our kids to live out their lives God knows where?"

"I wasn't sure," he said uncomfortably. "I kept thinking about the fact that you might have been sentenced to death. I hoped I could persuade you. I guess I snored sometimes when you were awake, but most nights I hardly slept at all. Do you think I could just go on living if that happened to you?"

"I never thought about it that way. Can you get the ten thousand back?"

"No. It was pay or play."

"Well . . ." She was silent for a while, and then she said, "We can afford it. You have to put it back in the partnership account."

"Yes—oh, absolutely."

She was silent for the next few minutes, and then she said, "I love you so, Billy—I just never loved you so much before, and you're very brave and wonderful; but you know, you're all of you little boys and you never grow up, all of you, Jack Ridley and Charley Anderson and Benson and even Haberman and all the rest of you, and my God, how this poor world has suffered from it! Don't be angry with me, Billy, but I have been through seven kinds of hell, and I feel connected with every woman on the face of the earth—and what are we to do? God help me, we are women, and this whole cursed abortion thing is a part of the war on women. Do you understand? Try to understand, because I need you. We have to do it together, women and men, and it's a long road to go."